THE DECKCHAIR DETECTIVES

Martin Oliver

Illustrated by Paddy Mounter

Designed by Paul Greenleaf

Contents

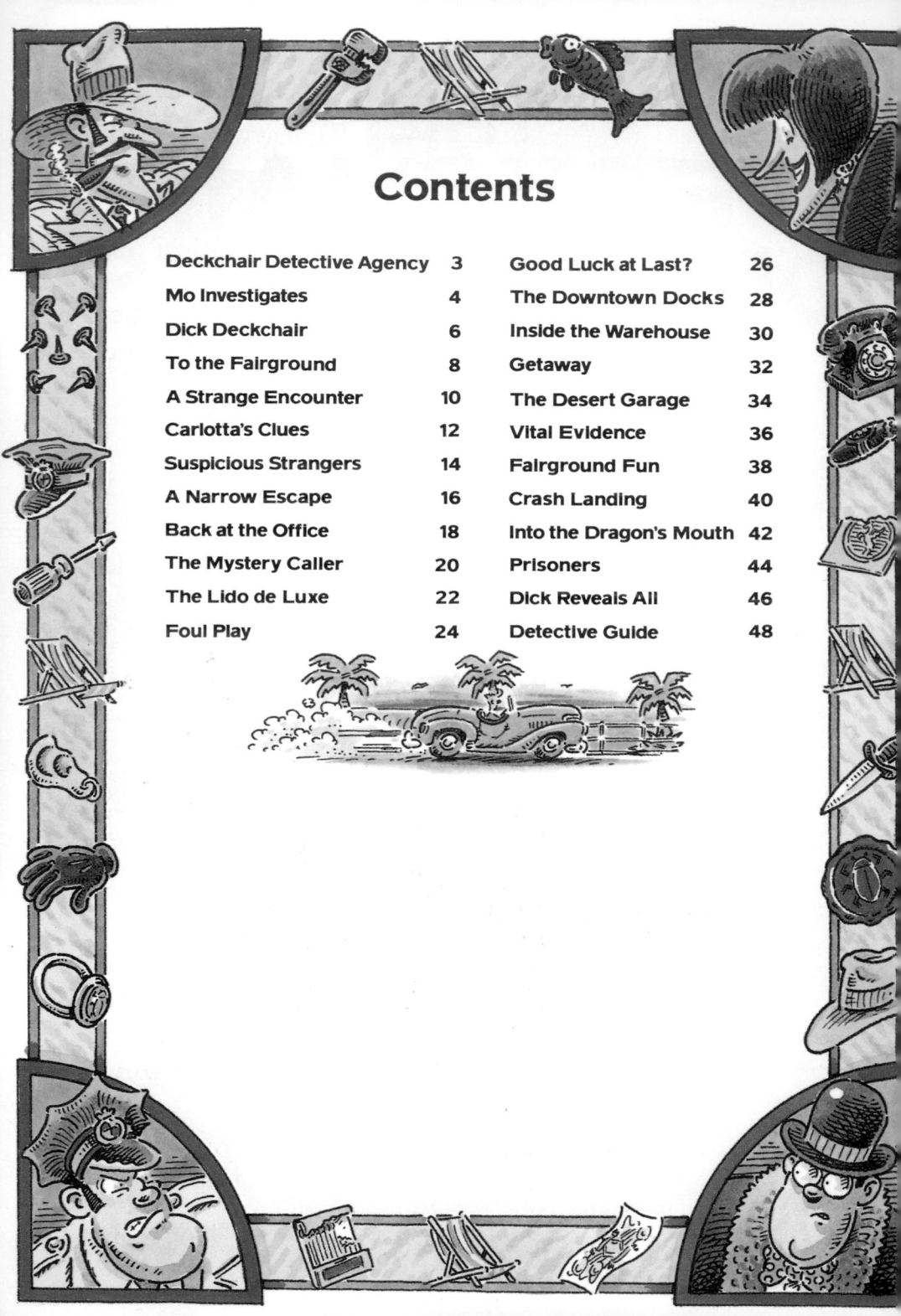

Deckchair Detective Agency

M o Jackson gulped and tried to control her jangling nerves as the ancient elevator clunked to a halt on the fourth floor of a grimy apartment building. She pushed the cage across and stepped out onto a dusty landing. Mo looked to her left and spotted the words 'Deckchair Detective Agency' on a glass door.

"Well, this is it. My big chance to become a detective," Mo thought as she glanced down to check the advertisement she had ripped out of a newspaper. "I may not have much experience, but at least I look the part in my supersleuth gear."

Mo stepped over to the door. She pushed her coat collar up, then tilted the brim of her hat down. Hoping that she looked more confident than she felt, Mo knocked on the door.

Mo Investigates

The door slowly creaked open a few inches. Mo hesitated for a second, waiting for someone to appear, but no one did. She shrugged her shoulders and stepped cautiously into the Deckchair Detective Agency. Her eyes opened wide with surprise.

The room was in chaos. Mo cast her private eye's eye over the mess. Her brain raced as she took in the overturned chair, the papers spilling out of drawers and the objects scattered across the floor. It looked as if the office had been ransacked.

"Hello, is anyone there?" she asked, but there was no reply. Sweat trickled down her face as a wave of warm, stale air wafted towards her. Overhead a ceiling fan whirred wearily, disturbing the top layer of dust and making the musty old papers flutter lazily. It was all very strange. Mo decided to investigate.

CREAK. A floorboard groaned as Mo walked up to the window. She stopped beside a filing cabinet. A large, hairy fly was buzzing angrily at the dirty pane of glass. Light filtered into the room through the broken slats of a grubby blind.

Ignoring a twinge of guilt, Mo began to flick through some of the yellowing papers inside the top drawer. She looked at the date on them and frowned – they were all ten years old or more. The contents of a lunch box didn't look much younger either. But just then, out of the corner of her eye, she spotted something that had been freshly made.

A trail of footprints in the dust led towards the back door. Who had made them? Was it an intruder? Was it the person who had ransacked the office? Mo had to find out.

She tiptoed up to the door and stopped in her tracks as she heard a strange sound coming from outside. What was it? Human without a doubt. There it was again, and again. It sounded like someone struggling for air. What was going on?

"This is it," Mo thought suddenly. "At last, a chance to prove myself as a private eye." In her mind she could see the headlines on tomorrow's front pages – *Detective unravels mystery of ransacked office.*

But what if there was a dangerous criminal outside? Mo gulped, then steeled herself for action. With a single bound she kicked open the door. "Come out with your hands up," she shouted. "We've got the place surrounded."

Dick Deckchair

A startled yell answered Mo's shout. It was followed by a crash and an ominous ripping sound. Mo stepped out onto a metal fire escape. She blinked her eyes in the bright sunlight and then focused on a bewildered looking figure who was staring back at her from underneath a broken deckchair.

Mo's shoulders slumped. Suddenly her coat felt much too big and far too hot. Her hat began to itch. She had been imagining things again. The person entangled in the deckchair didn't look much like a dangerous criminal and there was probably a perfectly normal explanation for the chaotic mess in the office.

A loud 'ouch' brought her attention back to the figure who was still trying to untangle himself from the remains of the deckchair. Mo helped him to his feet, then she introduced herself.

"Hello, I'm Mo Jackson. I'm looking for the Deckchair Detective Agency."

"You found it. I AM the agency. My name's Dick Deckchair."

"You don't look much like a detective."

"Of course I don't. If I did, everyone would know I was one. What do you want?"

"Er, I came about the job."

"That explains the fancy dress."

"I've just taken over the old family firm," Dick explained. "It's been a bit neglected but now I'm in charge, business is bound to boom. I'm determined to make it work. That's why I want an experienced detective to join me as a partner. What cases have you worked on?"

Mo admitted that she hadn't actually been involved in any cases yet. "But I know that I've got what it takes to be a detective," she said confidently. "If only I can have a chance."

"I don't know," Dick answered. "I'm a natural, you see. Just now I was taking a breather from office paperwork and polishing up my detecting techniques. You'd be amazed at the cases I've solved from my deckchair. The key to being a top 'tec is observation. You must always keep your eyes peeled and be on the alert for anything unusual."

"I agree, definitely," Mo replied. "Take that fire at the fairground for example. That's fairly unusual."

To the Fairground

Dick spun around. "Fire ...?" he spluttered, staring at the billowing plume of smoke in the distance. Then he recovered. "Well done," he blustered. "You've passed the first test. I was wondering when you'd spot that little spark."

Just then there was a loud knock at the office door. Dick looked startled. Then he grasped Mo's hand and gave it a firm shake.

"Welcome to the agency," he said. "Your first job is to answer the door." And with that, he shot off down the fire escape.

By now, Mo could hear heavy banging on the door. She didn't like the sound of it. "Hey," she shouted, racing after him. "Wait for me. What's the rush?"

"It's Great Aunt Bertha," he shouted over his shoulder as he shot off down the fire escape. "I'd recognize that knock anywhere..."

Dick was already behind the wheel of a battered jalopy when Mo jumped off the fire escape. He hit the accelerator. Mo clung on by her fingertips. She scrambled into the front seat then spotted a book on the floor. "How to be a good detective," Mo read aloud. "With pictures."

"OK, so neither of us are hot-shot detectives," Dick admitted. "But together we might make a good team. What do you say?"

"Maybe," said Mo. "First of all, let's check out that fire."

Minutes later the car bumped over rough wasteland and pulled up outside the fair. Dick and Mo got out and dashed up to the entrance. A plume of black smoke still hung in the air, but they couldn't see any flames. Maybe they were too late and had missed all the action.

"Come on," Mo said, ignoring the large sign by the entrance. "Let's go in and find out what's been going on."

They had just squeezed through the rusty turnstile when a dark shadow fell across their path. Dick looked up at a huge security guard blocking their way.

"Can't you read?" the guard snapped. "We're closed. Now scram."

Mo and Dick looked at each other. They weren't going to be pushed around by this bully. Then Dick had an idea. He fished into his pocket and pulled out his ID card. This should impress him, Dick thought.

It didn't. Dick and Mo gulped as heavy hands gripped their collars and their feet left the ground. Dick started to complain but his squeaky protests fell on deaf ears and he was lifted higher, legs kicking helplessly.

"I don't care if you're a deckchair detective or a defective deckchair," the guard snarled. "I've got my orders. You're not supposed to be here, and don't even think of coming back."

Dick and Mo tried to wriggle free of the iron grip, but the guard wouldn't let go. He was hauling the dangling detectives towards the exit when a throaty voice suddenly stopped him. "OK Tom. Put them down. I'll talk to them in my office."

A Strange Encounter

Mo looked around as her feet hit the floor. There was no sign of whoever had given the order, but the security guard was certainly obeying it. He pushed Dick and Mo down a narrow alley between The World of Wax and a shooting gallery. They stepped over power cables and ducked under steel girders then stopped at the back door of a tall building.

"This must be the office," Dick muttered. "Just keep quiet and let me handle this."

The door swung open and Dick and Mo were shoved inside. Dick's eyes opened wide at what he saw. He turned white and his legs wobbled. Mo turned to run, just as the door slammed shut. The sound of a key rattling in the lock echoed through the chamber.

"W..w..what sort of office is this?" Dick stuttered. "It's some sort of trap. We'll never get out of here." Mo shook her foot free of a mechanical arm and nearly tripped over something on the floor – it was a railway track. Her brain raced as she stared around the dingy dungeon. Suddenly it clicked. They were inside the Ghost Train.

Dick slowly turned less green once Mo told him what she had realized. He chuckled as he flicked the legs of a rubber spider. While he was making faces at a grinning skull, Mo spotted a newspaper lying on the blade of a plastic guillotine.

"Look at this," she said to Dick, brandishing the paper. "Both of these stories mention the fairground. It looks as though there have been other fires here before."

A DAUGHTER'S DESPERATE APPEAL

Tearful Viola Dodgem, daughter of missing ex-fairground owner, David Dodgem, appealed to the public for information that might lead to his whereabouts.

"He has been very nervous recently. He said he had discovered something important through an old fairground acquaintance."

FAIRGROUND FIRES

Since purchasing the city fairground one year ago, Carlotta Bottle has been dogged by bad luck. Although nobody has been hurt, two fires in last month have drastically reduced the number of visitors. Now Carlotta has spoken to THE GLOBE to assure customers that the fair is safe.

Dick peered over Mo's shoulder. He was still reading when he was interrupted by the sound of a cough and a throaty voice saying "Excuse me." Dick and Mo turned around and recognized the fairground owner who was sitting in a dimly lit corner.

"I hope my office didn't alarm you," said Carlotta Bottle, smiling as Dick shook his head decisively. "I am looking for a detective and you two might just be able to help me. I need you to find the person who is starting the fires at my fairground."

Carlotta's Clues

Mo's brain raced. This was it – their big chance! "We'd be delighted to help," she replied. "Efficiency, speed and success. That's our motto, isn't it Dick?"

"Er, yes definitely," Dick replied. "But are you sure the fires were started deliberately? Do you have any idea who might be behind them?"

"The culprit is David Dodgem – I'm sure of that," Carlotta answered. "But I don't know why he is doing it, or where he is hiding."

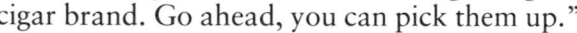

Carlotta emptied out a box file. "That's Dodgem," she said, pointing to two photos of a suspicious-looking character. "I wrote out a list of rides and took the other photos at the scene of the crime where I found the incriminating evidence – one of Dodgem's gloves and a butt of his usual cigar brand. Go ahead, you can pick them up."

While Dick and Mo examined the evidence, Carlotta stood up and yanked a piece of cord. A blind shot up revealing a window overlooking the fair.

"Dodgem used to own the fair until I took over a year ago," Carlotta breathed. "I know he's out there. He may still have accomplices working here."

"I know there's not much to go on, but you are my only hope. When you find him, let me know at once. No one else at the fair must know what you are doing..."

Just then Mo's ears pricked up as she heard a faint sound outside. She dashed over to the door and yanked it open. A familiar figure fell into the room. "Oh... hello Carlotta," the security guard stammered. "I was um... checking that these two weren't causing any trouble."

"Thanks for your concern Tom," Carlotta answered coldly. "But Dick and Mo are old friends of mine. What's the news on the latest fire?"

"It's bad, I'm afraid," Tom replied, shaking his head. "The Wall of Death is badly damaged and Max, the operator, has disappeared."

Dick stood up. It was time to investigate. A Deckchair Detective might find clues at the scene of a crime where an amateur would see nothing. As he and Mo turned to leave, Carlotta scribbled on a piece of paper and pressed it into Mo's hand. "This is my number," she explained. "Contact me when you have news."

They stepped outside and set off in search of the Wall of Death. "Follow me," Dick said. "And don't forget what Carlotta said – Dodgem might still have accomplices here. Stay alert, keep your eyes and ears open."

Dick walked down past the side of the Hall of Mirrors. Mo was right beside him, when all of a sudden she stopped dead in her tracks.

"Listen," she hissed pointing to a window behind her. Dick and Mo strained their ears and heard a man's voice whispering. What he was saying sounded very suspicious. Dick tiptoed up to the window and peered inside.

Max had it coming to him. He was sticking his nose into our business. He must have found the entrance mechanism.

13

Suspicious Strangers

(5) Dick's eyes boggled at what he saw, then he realized he was looking at distorted reflections of three people. He couldn't see their faces clearly, but he understood what the trio were saying. They had disposed of Max, but who were they? Who was 'the boss' and who was 'Sharkey'?

Dick and Mo needed to get a closer look at the strange trio. They were creeping up to the front of the Hall of Mirrors when a strangely-clad apparition materialized in a cloud of smoke and blocked their way. "Who... who are you?" Dick asked, astonished.

"I am Clare Voyant," the figure replied. "I see danger before you. Be on your guard." As she finished speaking, the woman wrapped her cape around her and disappeared in a swirl of purple, leaving a faint smell of violets, and Dick and Mo open-mouthed with amazement.

"Come on Dick," Mo whispered, snapping herself back to attention. "I'm not letting some old phoney frighten us off the case, we've still got to get a good look at those three characters in the mirrors."

They crept inside the Hall of Mirrors, but it was empty. The strange trio had disappeared without trace, or had they? Dick spotted a scrap of paper on the floor. The message on it was strange, and so was the wax seal. What was it all about? Dick had a hunch it might be useful in the future. He put it in his pocket and (6) they headed for the Wall of Death.

Congratulations on carrying out your task today. You're needed for the shift tonight. Another consignment must be ready at the docks by midnight. Watch out for Sharkey and his mob.

14

Minutes later, Dick stared up at the smouldering remains of the ride. The air was still thick with the smell of burning wood, and ash was gently drifting down onto the scorched earth. Dick kept a safe distance from the damaged ride and bent down to check the ground for clues. Nothing. He straightened up just in time to see Mo disappear through the main doors.

"There may be some evidence inside," she shouted. "Keep an eye open while I go in and investigate."

Before Dick could stop her, Mo was gone. Dick looked around uneasily. Out of the corner of his eye he glimpsed a purple shadow, but then it was gone. A sudden gust of wind made the rickety structure groan and sway. A piece of wood clattered to the ground, followed by another, then another. Dick shouted out a desperate warning.

Look out!

15

A Narrow Escape

D ick raced up to the Wall of Death but he tripped over an empty bucket and went flying, just as the structure sagged slightly to the left and collapsed with a thundering crash. Dick kept his head down. As soon as the last lethal fragment of flying debris had whistled past his ears, he staggered up and wobbled over to find Mo.

A pile of shattered planks moved, then coughed. Mo opened her eyes and sat up shakily. "I'm fine," she spluttered to Dick. "But I think we'd better get going before anyone finds us here. We're supposed to be working undercover."

Dick glanced over his shoulder. Fairground workers were heading over to what had once been the Wall of Death, and none of them looked very happy. Dick dragged Mo out of the wreckage.

"Come on, let's go" Mo panted. She leaned against Dick for support and they half-staggered, half-sprinted away. As Mo gradually recovered, they accelerated to increase the distance between themselves and the angry shouts behind. "Why did you go into that death trap?" Dick asked. as they dashed around a corner. "Don't tell me you found some important evidence in that ruin."

SMACK. Before Mo could answer she crashed straight into Tom. She lay on the floor, winded as the security guard towered over them.

"I thought I'd already told you two to scram," he hissed angrily. Then his voice softened. "It's dangerous here. If anyone else had found you, it would have been curtains. You must leave."

Tom pointed down a passageway that ran between a row of trailers and some power generators. "Head that way, take the third opening on the left and you'll find a gap in the fence. Now get out of here."

They went. Mo was first under the wire and into the car. Dick gunned the motor and they sped back to the office. They had seen and heard so many strange things that Dick was beginning to suspect there was more to the case than had first met the eye.

Dick turned off the main road and a few minutes later arrived at Seaview Mansions. He was stepping out of the car when he noticed that Mo's left hand was tightly clenched.

"So, did you find anything inside the Wall of Death?" he asked.

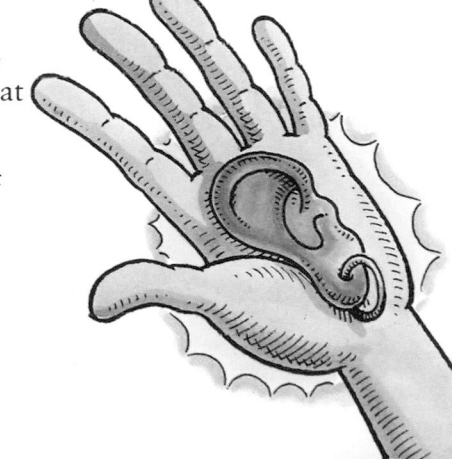

There was a second's pause, then Dick watched as Mo slowly loosened her grip to reveal what she had found.

Back at the Office

Mo held out the ear for a closer look but Dick backed away and jumped out of the car. He crashed into a burly man who was hurrying past. Dick mumbled an apology but the man just picked up what he had dropped and walked on without speaking.

Mo helped Dick into the cranky elevator. She hit the fourth-floor button and they clanked jerkily upward. Mo held out the ear again. "It's not real," she said. "I think it must come from a wax figure at the fairground. I found it inside the cashbox belonging to Max, the operator."

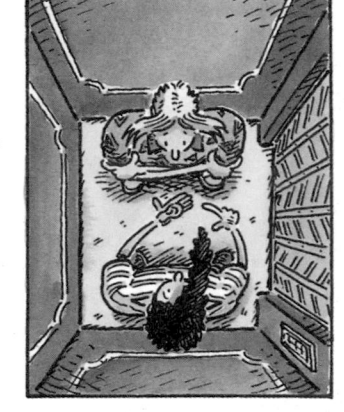

"It's a very strange thing to keep in a cashbox," Dick said, idly thinking back to the conversation he had overheard in the Hall of Mirrors. "Max must have thought it was important. I wonder if it's connected with..."

Dick never finished as the elevator suddenly shuddered to an abrupt halt at the fourth floor. Mo pocketed the ear while Dick staggered out of the elevator and unlocked the office door. They both stepped inside.

Mo produced a pen and notebook. "I have a hunch that if we are going to find Dodgem we must investigate everything we've seen and heard so far. The ear, the note with the wax seal, the strange trio, Sharkey..."

"That name rings a bell," Dick interrupted. "I'm sure I saw something on him in the batch of 'S' files I tidied up earlier. Where are they?"

Dick had just found the 'S' drawer when there was a knock on the door. "I'll get it," Mo volunteered. She opened the door, just in time to hear footsteps clattering down the stairs below. Then she spotted a brown envelope on the door mat. "I wonder what's in it," Mo muttered.

"Let's find out," Dick replied. As he cleared a space on the top of the desk and began to unfasten the flap of the envelope, his nostrils twitched. There was a faint smell that reminded him of something, of flowers. He shrugged and pulled out the contents.

There is more to the case than you have been told. I found this book of matches by the Wall of Death

A friend —.

Mo examined the photograph and the matches, then she read the handwritten message. "Very mysterious," she said. "I wonder who this person is in the photo? And who is 'a friend'?"

Dick scratched his head. The case was certainly getting more and more complicated, but they were no closer to finding Dodgem. "What do you think we should do now?" he asked, but before Mo could answer the telephone rang.

"Deckchair Detective Agency. How can we help?" Dick said, picking up the receiver.

Dick heard a woman's voice. Mo moved closer and they listened intently to what the caller said, but before they could speak, she hung up. Would she call back? They had to wait . .

This is a friend. Look at the contents of the envelope. I can't speak now in case the call is traced. I will call back with vital information.

The Mystery Caller

The Deckchair Detectives waited inside the office.

Then the phone rang.

Dick grabbed the receiver.

Hello. Who is this?

It is too dangerous to reveal my identity. I delivered the envelope to you.

The mystery caller was speaking from a nearby phone booth.

If you want to find out more about the fairground fires, then listen carefully. I will say this only once.

Meanwhile, inside a darkened room not very far from Seaview Mansions, unfriendly ears were listening in on the mysterious telephone call. As Mo edged closer to the receiver, she and Dick were unaware that a tape recorder was whirring slowly, recording every word. Clearly they were not the only ones interested in the mystery caller...

This matter extends beyond the fairground. The fires are just the tip of a dangerous iceberg. Do you have the photograph I sent you?

Please go on. We're all ears.

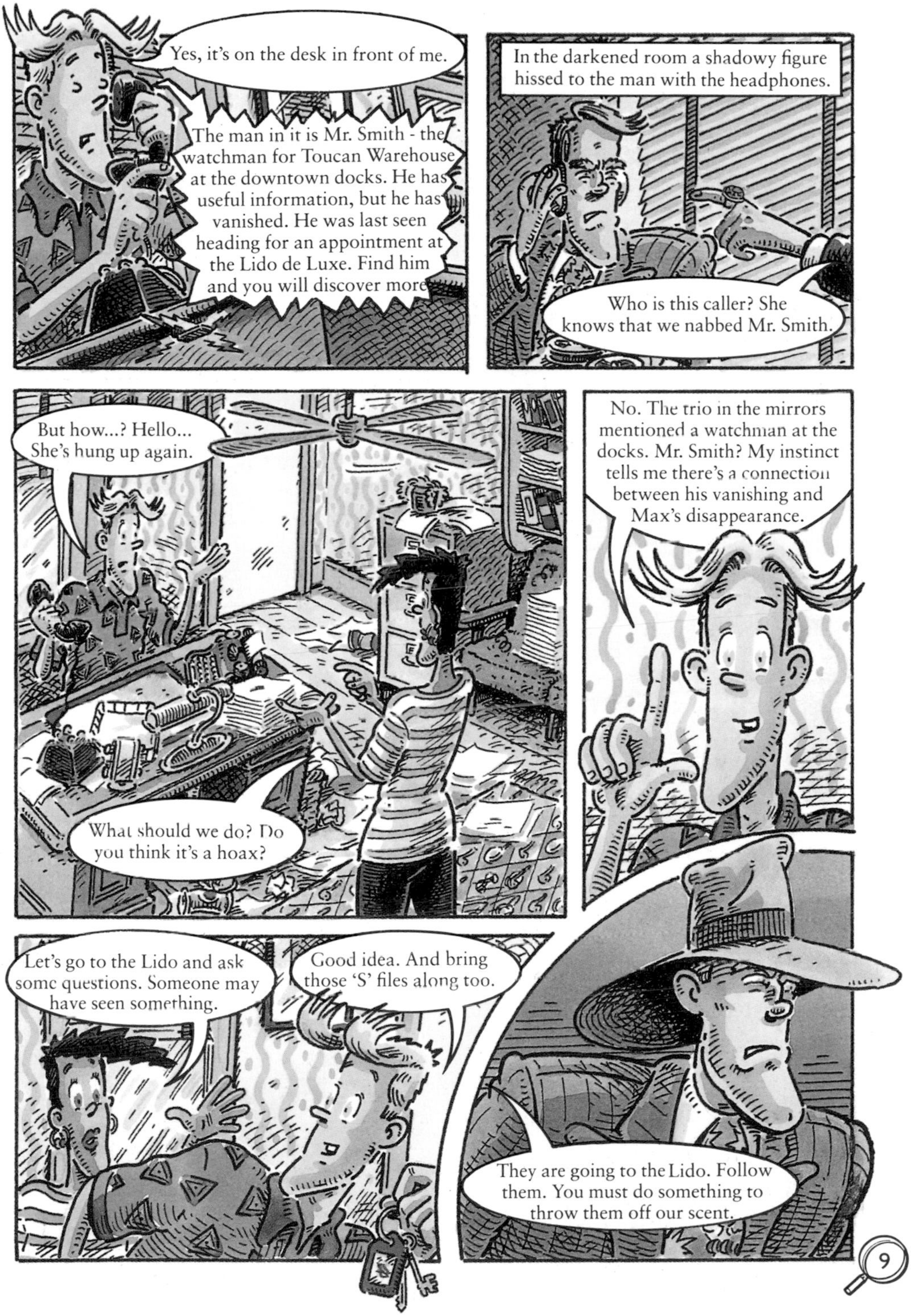

Panel 1:

Yes, it's on the desk in front of me.

The man in it is Mr. Smith - the watchman for Toucan Warehouse at the downtown docks. He has useful information, but he has vanished. He was last seen heading for an appointment at the Lido de Luxe. Find him and you will discover more.

Panel 2:

In the darkened room a shadowy figure hissed to the man with the headphones.

Who is this caller? She knows that we nabbed Mr. Smith.

Panel 3:

But how...? Hello... She's hung up again.

What should we do? Do you think it's a hoax?

Panel 4:

No. The trio in the mirrors mentioned a watchman at the docks. Mr. Smith? My instinct tells me there's a connection between his vanishing and Max's disappearance.

Panel 5:

Let's go to the Lido and ask some questions. Someone may have seen something.

Good idea. And bring those 'S' files along too.

Panel 6:

They are going to the Lido. Follow them. You must do something to throw them off our scent.

9

The Lido de Luxe

Dick drove to the Lido, dodging and weaving through the traffic. The breeze ruffled Mo's hair and cleared her head as she ran through her notes on the facts of the case. "There have been three fires at the fairground and we know that Max, the operator of the Wall of Death is missing. We overheard three villains at the fairground, but we don't know who they are. There's also something going on at the docks, and then there's our mystery caller who told us that someone else – a watchman at the docks – is missing."

"We've got a glove and a cigar butt belonging to Dodgem," Mo continued. "They were both found by Carlotta at the scene of the first two fires. There's also the note with the strange seal and the ear. Then we have a torn book of matches sent by our mystery caller and the photograph of Mr. Smith. What does it all add up to?"

Dick shrugged, regained control of the car and pulled up beside some wrought iron gates. They spotted the Lido through the bushes, but they failed to notice the sinister figure watching their every move...

Dick tried to open the gates, only to find they were locked. "That's no problem, follow me," Mo said, squeezing through the railings. A few tugs, yanks and ouches later, Dick joined her and they crept into the Lido. Mo whistled in amazement as she reached the poolside. She could see why it was called the Lido de Luxe, but now what? There was no one around to answer questions about Mr. Smith, the missing watchman.

"Just keep your eyes peeled for any clues or evidence that might prove Mr. Smith was here," Dick whispered.

Mo checked through the foliage beside the pool and sighed. This was pointless, she didn't even know what she should be looking for. She turned around and spotted a sudden movement by a statue. But before she could focus properly she was distracted by Dick's loud gasp.

Foul Play

Before Mo could move, Dick jumped into the pool. A few tense seconds later his head broke through the surface as he struggled to keep a hold on the heavy, water-logged figure.

"Give me a hand," gasped Dick, swimming to the side. Mo reached down and heaved the body out of the pool.

Gasping for air, Dick clambered out of the water. "Tell me the worst," he said, wiping his eyes. "How bad is he?"

"See for yourself," Mo answered.

Dick slowly looked down. The drowned man was a statue!

"That's where it came from," Mo said, pointing to a damaged pedestal. "And this looks very much like Mr. Smith's hat."

"I'm beginning to suspect foul play," Dick muttered as he dripped his way over to Mo. "All the evidence here points to a struggle in which Mr. Smith's hat was crushed and the statue was knocked off its pedestal."

"If my deduction is correct, that leaves us with one vital question to answer," Dick continued. "Who was Mr. Smith's assailant?"

"What about this?" Mo asked, picking up a black glove. "It's a perfect match with the one Carlotta found. Dodgem seems to be getting very careless."

CRACK. The sound of a twig snapping rang through the night air like a gunshot. Dick dived for cover. "Get up," hissed Mo. "Someone's out there, hiding in the bushes. Let's get them."

Dick went left, Mo headed right. Eyes straining and hearts pounding, they crashed through bushes and ducked under branches, chasing after the shadowy figure ahead.

Mo stopped suddenly. She had lost the figure in the darkness, or had she? Over there! Mo pounced. At that moment Dick spotted someone heading straight for him. "Got you," he yelled launching himself into a tackle. "OUCH."

Mo and Dick staggered unsteadily to their feet. A sudden gust of wind parted the clouds in the evening sky and the park was flooded with moonlight. Mo spotted a dark outline dash out of the bushes and sprint over to the gates.

They set off at top speed, but by the time they reached the entrance the mystery figure had scaled the gates and been swallowed up by the night. Dick and Mo heard a car start, then screech around a distant corner.

"Who was that man, and what was he doing here?" Dick mused. "Now we'll never know. Whoever he was has escaped."

"But he's left part of his jacket on the spikes," Mo replied. "Let's get it down. It might be useful."

Good Luck at Last?

Dick yanked impatiently at the torn jacket. The material held firm for a second then suddenly it was free. Dick knelt down as a stream of objects fell out of a pocket. Mo switched on the car headlights and joined Dick. "Look at all this," Dick exclaimed, as he examined their finds. "I have a feeling our luck is about to change. Something here must help us with the case."

12

Can you fit a face to the master criminal who runs the city? This is an artist's impression of what the villain may look like, but one knows the identity of this powerful boss. Can you help? It is rumoured that the super villain has an almost supernatural ability to predict police movements and

THE GLOBE

SHOCK

An undercover police officer and Bookham escort person

ALIENS IN ALBATRAZ?
After reports of lights flickering in the derelict jail, Albatraz, we took this photo of a UFO. Is this proof at last that alien beings hav

Clare Voyant
Your future is my future

Dick's brain was racing. He was sure he had seen something or someone in the photo before, but he felt so muddled that he couldn't put the pieces into place. "We need more information," he muttered. "But where can we get it?"

"Search me," answered Mo, then suddenly she remembered something. She reached into the car and unlocked the glove compartment. "These are the 'S' files you told me to bring from the office," she said. "Look! Here's something on Sharkey, and what about the picture on this document? It's identical to the seal on the note we found in the Hall of Mirrors."

"That's brilliant," Dick grinned. "We're getting somewhere at last. Once we've read everything, let's check out the downtown docks."

13

The Downtown Docks

Dick cut the engine and turned off the headlights. The car rolled to a silent halt in a dark alley beside Toucan Warehouse. Dick peered down at the dashboard clock – it was two minutes to midnight. Staying in the shadows, Mo crept to the corner of the warehouse and stared around.

The loading doors at the front of the building were brightly lit by overhead street lamps. Apart from a scavenging cat, the docks were deserted. All was quiet except for the slapping of water against the sea wall and the chugging of a distant boat out in the bay.

"There doesn't seem to be anybody around," Mo whispered. She stepped back into the shadows and sat down by an overflowing bin. Dick yawned hugely and began flicking a coin.

It was spinning in mid air when Dick heard a match striking. Light flared up at a window in the warehouse opposite. The flickering flame illuminated an instantly recognizable silhouette – Dodgem!

Dick gasped. The coin hit the floor with a clank. Dick grabbed Mo's shoulder and pointed her to the window, but Dodgem was gone. Dick rubbed his eyes. It had happened so quickly, maybe he had been dreaming? There was only one way to find out.

Dick and Mo sped across to the warehouse and flattened themselves against one of the locked doors. Mo pressed her ear against the thick wood. She could just make out the dull murmur of heavy machinery. "We must get in and find out what Dodgem's up to," hissed Dick. "But how?"

Mo spotted a way up to the first floor. "Don't make a sound," she hissed. "I'm going in."

Dick watched as Mo clambered up some crates, swung onto an open loading door and knelt on a narrow window ledge. "Come on," she whispered. "It's your turn, I'll give you a hand." Dick gulped then shinned up a drainpipe and joined Mo on the ledge. They slipped silently through the open door, crept along a dusty corridor to a balcony and peered down. There was no sign of Dodgem, but the characters below looked vaguely familiar. Dick wracked his brains, but he couldn't figure out where he had seen them before.

14

Inside the Warehouse

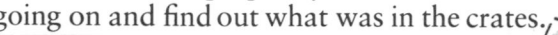

What were they doing down there? Dick and Mo had to get a closer look, but how? They were bound to be spotted. They needed a diversion.

Outside, a ship's whistle blew twice. Right on cue the machinery was turned off, then two men opened the doors and began picking up the crates. Dick and Mo crept quietly downstairs. Now they could discover what was going on and find out what was in the crates.

 "Deckchairs," Dick muttered in surprise, levering open a wooden lid.

"Money," gasped Mo, as she thrust her hand deeper into the crate and pulled out the top layer under the straw packaging. The gang members were forgers! "So that's what the dockside operation is all about," Mo said grabbing a wad of the counterfeit money. "I'll just take this as evidence."

"We must search the warehouse thoroughly," Mo continued. "We've got to find Dodgem again." Dick nodded eagerly and they crept past a small office. Suddenly they heard the screech of brakes outside, followed by loud shouts and the pounding of feet. Dick and Mo hit the deck as a burst of gunfire sent bullets whizzing over their heads.

Dick's heart pounded as he waited for the order, "Come out with your hands up." But it never came. Instead he and Mo heard crashes, bangs and angry yells. Cautiously they peered out from their hiding place.

The docks were in chaos. The counterfeiters were being attacked by a bunch of gangsters wearing sharp suits and hats. Mo recognized the leader of the second group – holding a megaphone and shouting instructions to his men was Sharkey. The realization of what was happening suddenly struck her. "We're in the middle of a gang war," she breathed in disbelief. "This is amazing."

"This is a disaster," Dick said, tugging at her shoulder. "Let's get out of here while we're still in one piece."

Getaway

As stray bullets ricocheted around their ears, Mo agreed it was time to go. She had taken two paces when Dick gasped. Mo turned to see him frantically dabbing at red stains on his shirt.

"I... I'm hit," Dick quavered. "Go on without me." But Mo just smiled and pointed to a bullet-ridden can of red paint dripping from the shelf above.

Gingerly, Dick checked himself for bullet holes then followed Mo in her search for an escape route. While the rival gangs were still battling each other on the waterfront, Mo spotted a side door. She tried the handle. With a sigh of relief she discovered it was unlocked.

Mo pushed the door open and peered out. Their car was parked a few feet away. She stared around, the coast was clear. Dick and Mo dashed across the alley and dived into the car. Dick fumbled for his keys.

"Please start," Dick begged. "Please."

The engine choked, spluttered and died. Dick groaned loudly. Behind them came an angry yell. They had been spotted!

Dick desperately turned the key again. Pistol shots rang out from behind them. Suddenly the windscreen shattered and cracked. "Get down," Dick hissed. "Here we go – this is our last chance."

VROOOOM. The engine roared into life at last. Dick stepped on the accelerator. The wheels screeched and the car shot off down the narrow alley. Up ahead was a brick wall! Dick yanked on the brake and they took the left-hand turn on two wheels. Mo opened her eyes as they bounced back onto solid ground. They were still alive, and Toucan Warehouse was receding into the distance.

Dick checked his rearview mirror. No one was on their tail. He eased off the gas, took a left turn and headed back into town. "So now we know what Dodgem is mixed up with," he began. "I bet Mr. Smith disappeared because he stumbled on the counterfeiting racket."

"I agree," Mo answered. "But I've been racking my brains and there's still one thing I don't understand. What's the connection between Dodgem and the fairground fires?"

Dick groaned, he didn't know either. They were still miles away from wrapping up the case. As Dick tried to see a way through the muddle of confusing evidence, a car pulled up at the lights beside them. Dick sniffed the air and wrinkled up his nose at the bitter smell of cigar smoke. He glanced across and gasped as he recognized the driver – it was Dodgem!

"Stay on his tail," Mo hissed. The lights changed. Dodgem accelerated ahead and Dick followed. Then, Dodgem turned off the main road and bumped down dusty side tracks. The miles sped by and the sun beat down. "This is easy," Dick thought. "Dodgem obviously hasn't spotted..."

Dick never finished. Up ahead Dodgem accelerated quickly. As Dick changed into overdrive a blue car screamed past. Mo saw a hand reach out of the car and drop rusty nails on the road ahead. "Look out," she shouted, but it was too late.

Dick slammed on the brakes and wrestled with the wheel as they screeched to a punctured halt. Dick and Mo could only watch as Dodgem and the other car sped off in a cloud of dust.

The Desert Garage

The dejected duo slowly climbed out of the car to inspect the damage. The groan of cooling metal and the hiss of escaping air was accompanied by Dick sighing. The car was beyond repair. There was only one thing to do – walk for help. But which way? There was no traffic or any other sign of life in either direction.

"We may as well head in the same direction as Dodgem," Mo said.

Dick trudged along after Mo. The blistering sun blazed down on them and clouds of dust scratched at their throats, making them cough and choke. Dick and Mo toiled on, occasionally stopping to rest in the shade of a prickly roadside cactus. Dick fanned his face as a blast of hot air burned into his lungs. "Let's stop," he croaked, licking his cracked lips. "We're not getting anywhere like this."

A snake slithered out of the way as Dick sat down by the side of the road. Mo stared hard into the heat haze ahead and spotted something shimmering in the distance... Was it a mirage? No, it was a garage.

Dick caught up with Mo a few paces later. "I hope it's not deserted," said Mo, scanning the peeling paintwork on the ramshackle building. "It's not exactly the busiest road in the world."

"Hello," Dick shouted, racing ahead. "Anyone there?"

Nothing disturbed the silence except for a lizard scurrying up a wooden post and the squeak of a door swinging on rusty hinges. Then, as they walked closer, they heard faint voices coming from behind a dusty window. Dick froze as he recognized one of the voices and tried to make out what they were saying, but Mo wasn't paying attention.

"We're in luck," Mo said, and before Dick could stop her, she rapped on the glass. The sound of voices stopped abruptly then a figure appeared in the doorway. It was Tom, the fairground security guard! What was he doing here?

"Not you two again," Tom groaned as he recognized Dick and Mo. "Come here," he snapped impatiently. "We've got some serious talking to do."

"No way," shouted Dick, grabbing Mo's arm and pulling her out of Tom's reach. "Run for it."

Dick and Mo sprinted past heaps of rusting car parts. Mo looked over her shoulder and gasped, Tom was close behind them and getting closer. Just then he launched himself into a flying tackle. Quick as a flash, Mo swung an old car seat around to block him. To her amazement, Tom landed on a spring and went flying...

Vital Evidence

Mo checked to see if Tom was all right. He was out for the count and snoring loudly. That left the other person Tom had been talking to, whoever that might be.

Just then an engine roared. Dick spun around and saw a familiar car speeding down the road. He recognized the driver at once. Dodgem was getting away. Dick aimed a sharp stone at the car's back wheel. It missed and bounced harmlessly into a ditch.

Dick hurried back to the garage. Tom was still sleeping peacefully, but where was Mo? A shout from a doorway led Dick into a small untidy room. Mo looked up from a pile of papers and photos on a table top.

"This is Dodgem's hideout," she said excitedly. "Tom must be his accomplice at the fairground. Things are falling into place now. Look at the wax seals on the messages – it's the Scarab Society again, and this is the plate which they use to forge money. These photos look like pictures of their criminal activities. I wonder why they took them?"

Max is getting dangerous. He's found our secret in the Dragon Temple and wants to talk. A torch job should do the trick. I shall personally take great pleasure in supplying the match, then we shall take him to our secret headquarters. Mr Smith has also been snooping around too much. He must be dealt with. Arrange rendezvous trap and then take him to join Max for a long island holiday.

URGENT
I have just received a tip-off from an informer. Our dockside operation is no longer safe from Sharkey. One final batch of money must be made up tonight, then use the boat to transfer everything to our secret headquarters.

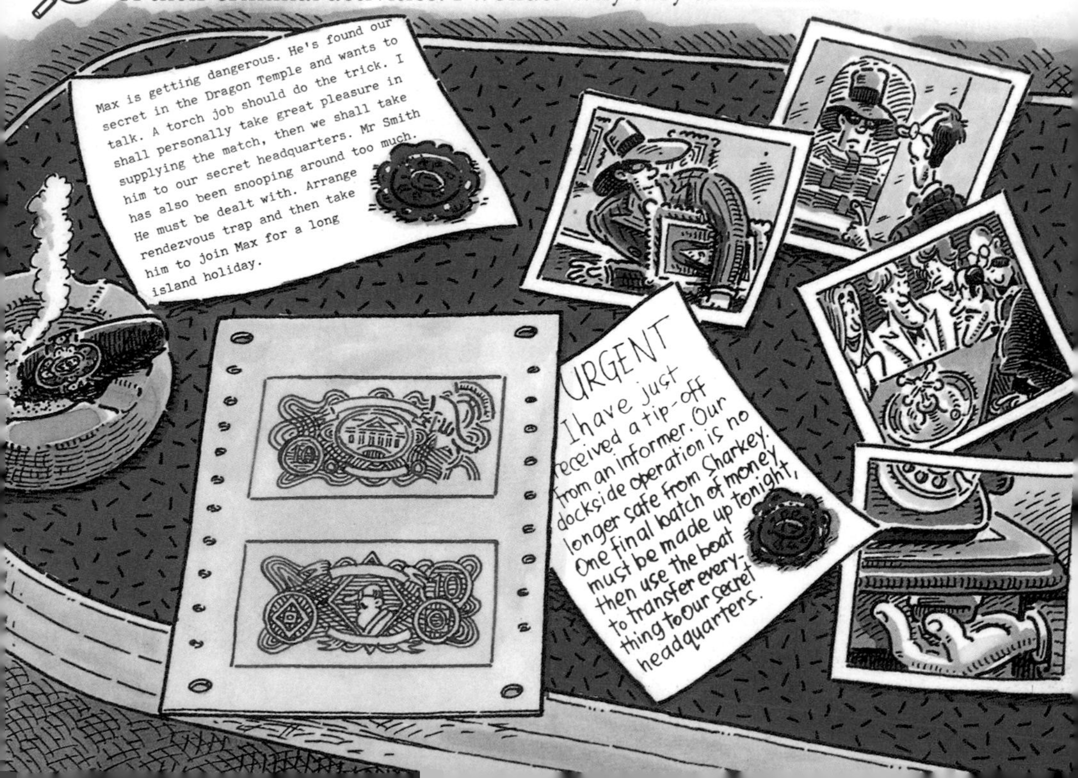

Mo's question wasn't the only nagging doubt in Dick's mind. It looked as if Dodgem was the leader of the Scarab Society, but as he examined the evidence, Dick felt he was missing something.

"Let's contact Carlotta," Mo continued. "Here's her number." A distant alarm sounded in Dick's head when he saw the scrap of paper Mo was holding, but he didn't know why. In the meantime, Mo phoned Carlotta and told her what they had discovered.

Well done. Bring the plates and the evidence to the fairground. Why don't we meet in my office at dawn.

The fairground owner seemed pleased with the news. Mo listened to Carlotta's suggestion and had just agreed to meet her when CLICK, the line went dead. What was going on? Dick spotted Tom lurching their way, wire cutters in hand. Dick gulped and turned white while Mo stuffed the evidence in a green folder. She grabbed Dick and they both dived out of the back window.

Mo picked herself up from the dust and stared around frantically. "This way," she shouted, heading for Tom's car. She yanked open the door and reached for the ignition... there were no keys. What should they do now? Mo moved out of the way as Dick crouched low beneath the steering wheel and fumbled with the casing. Seconds later, the engine coughed then spluttered to life.

Dick spun the wheel. The car swerved around Tom, hit a fuel pump, then bounced and jolted onto the road. As they headed back into town, Mo turned to watch Tom become a smaller and smaller dot on the horizon.

"Where did you learn that trick?" Mo asked in amazement.

"From a villain called Hotwire Harry," Dick replied sheepishly. "I had a hunch that it might come in useful one day."

Fairground Fun

Dick and Mo arrived at the moonlit fairground just after five o'clock in the morning. Dick was feeling apprehensive. He wasn't sure why, but vague worries had been lurking at the back of his mind ever since they had discovered Dodgem's hideout. Perhaps they should be looking at this case from another angle . . .

"Come on," Mo hissed, pushing Dick through the turnstile and following him into the fair. Silver moonlight threw sharp, stabbing shadows onto the ground and made the roller coaster look like a huge iron skeleton. "This is spooky," whispered Dick as they made their way past the helter-skelter.

Just then, neon lights around them began to hum and buzz. Mo's face turned pink while Dick took on a greenish hue. "H . . . hello, who . . . who's there?" stammered Dick. "Is that you Carlotta?"

Hand over the evidence.

Do as we say.

Then no one will get hurt.

Three figures stepped out of the shadows and hissed out orders. Mo instantly recognized the villains' faces from the warehouse. With a sickening lurch in his stomach, Dick realized he had heard their voices before. The villains were the strange trio from the Hall of Mirrors. A question flashed through his mind. How did these villains know that Dick and Mo would be at the fairground tonight? But the only thought in Mo's head was escape. She had already spotted a way out. She grabbed Dick and they ripped through a coconut shy. Dick snatched at some coconuts and wrenched one free from its pole.

 22

As Dick dashed after Mo something whistled past his shoulder. They turned around as knives cut through the air and sliced into the wooden boarding behind, quivering where they landed. Liquid trickled over Dick's hand. "I knew that coconut would come in handy," he thought.

Dick and Mo ran for their lives, jumping over ropes, dodging past the bumper cars and weaving through the waltzers, until they reached the exit. But it was guarded by one of the trio holding a lighted torch.

The villain lifted a bottle to his lips. Mo could smell fuel. Suddenly she realized what was about to happen. "DUCK," she yelled.

They dived for cover as a tongue of bright orange flame whooshed up to them, spitting angrily and scorching everything in its path.

Apart from singed eyebrows, Mo and Dick were unhurt. Before the human flame thrower could reload, they were back on their feet. They sprinted past the Big Dipper and headed for the roller coaster.

"Get into one of the cars," Dick ordered. He hit the 'on' switch and jumped in beside her. The car rocketed along the rails, taking Mo's breath away.

Behind them the two villains were about to follow but they stared along the track and changed their minds. Dick glanced ahead. Horror-struck, he knew what the third villain had been doing . . .

Crash Landing

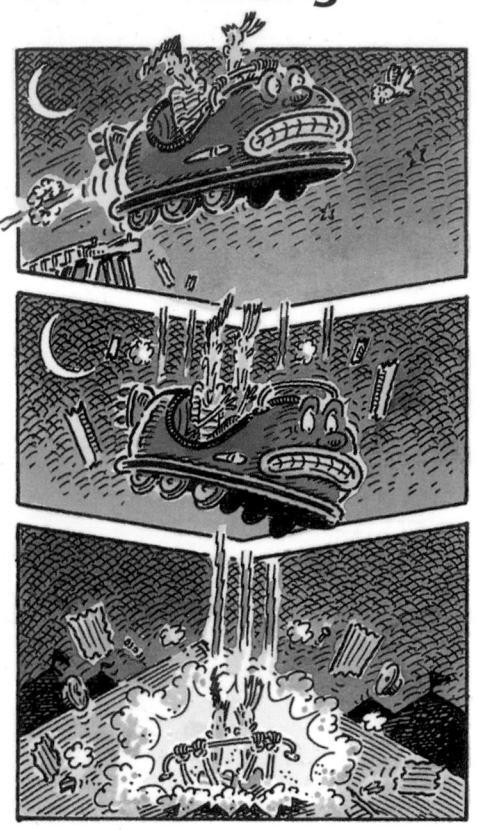

Dick's desperate shout hung in the air as the car hit the broken track and flew off into the night. Mo's life flashed quickly before her eyes while Dick's cry choked off into a strangled scream.

They raced up through the night sky and for a few seconds all was quiet apart from the wind whistling through their hair. The car hovered for a moment and then began plummeting to the ground. Dick stared through his fingers in horror – they were heading for one of the shows.

CRASH. Splinters flew and glass shattered as the car smashed through the roof of the fairground show. It bounced once before collapsing into pieces. Mo and Dick felt every bone in their body shudder, then blackness descended.

The dust began to settle on Dick and Mo, who were out cold. As they lay dazed among the rubble, they were unaware that the three villains were heading to where the car had crash-landed. Meanwhile, above Dick and Mo's heads, a sliver of wood swayed from a shattered rafter. It broke free and clattered to the floor.

"What's going on?" Dick groaned. "Ouch!" Brightly tinted stars spun around his head but they soon disappeared as he remembered the knives, the flame and then the crash. He was all right, what about Mo? "Are you OK?" he hissed.

"I'll be fine," Mo answered groggily. "Just tell me what hit us and where we are."

Dick staggered unsteadily to his feet and stared around. He blinked twice and waited for his sight to return to normal. He rubbed his eyes again, but the strange figures and Chinese decorations wouldn't go away. Then it dawned on him – this was the Dragon Temple.

Mo gasped. In a flash she remembered that the Dragon Temple was mentioned in one of the notes with the scarab seal, but before she could tell Dick, she caught the sound of a door opening, followed by heavy footsteps. "We've got visitors," she said. "And I don't think they've come to ask about our health. Let's get out of here."

Mo grabbed Dick's arm, but he wouldn't move. He was staring at one of the wax figures. Mo suddenly realized why . . . the guard's right ear was missing. Mo fumbled in her pockets and held up the ear she had found in the Wall of Death – it was a perfect match.

Into the Dragon's Mouth

Mo spotted a red button sticking out of the side of the wax figure's head. The broken ear fitted perfectly into position. "Stand back," Mo whispered, pressing hard on the button. There was a loud click, followed by the sound of cogwheels grinding. Dick jumped as the dragon's jaw sprang open with a loud clang. He peered into the open mouth, and could just see a flight of steps leading down into a dark tunnel.

Mo heard sounds of the three villains behind. "Let's go," she said, pushing Dick into the tunnel. As they stumbled down the steps, the entrance snapped shut behind them. There was no going back now.

Dick took the green folder and put it in his pocket as Mo dug out a box of matches. By the light of the flickering flame they crept cautiously forwards.

"I guess this is an old smuggler's tunnel," whispered Dick. "But where does it lead?"

They didn't have to wait too long to find out. Ten matches later the tunnel ended at a solid wall of stone. Mo spotted footholds, cut into the rock, leading up to a small wooden trap door.

(23)

Dick looked on as Mo planted her feet securely in the footholds and pushed against the trap door with all her strength. It opened a few reluctant inches, letting shafts of light pierce the gloom below. Mo paused for a second. Where would they come out?

Mo lifted the trapdoor higher and looked around. They were in some sort of courtyard. Half-ruined watch towers jutted up into the sky while coils of rusting wire sprawled over the grass. This was Albatraz, the abandoned city jail. The tunnel had led Dick and Mo under the sea and out onto the island prison.

"At least we know why Max disappeared," hissed Dick, crawling out beside Mo. "It all ties in with that typed note we found in Dodgem's hideout and what the trio said in the Hall of Mirrors. Max must have stumbled on the tunnel entrance. He took the ear as evidence, but the Scarab Society got wind of him and torched his ride."

"You're right, but why is the tunnel such a big secret?" Mo tried one of the steel doors that led from the courtyard into the main building – it was unlocked. The door swung open silently and Dick and Mo peered into a deserted hall. Then they spotted the two prisoners and the scarab flags. This had to be the Scarab Society headquarters.

Prisoners

Dick and Mo dashed over to the surprised prisoners. Dick recognized Mr. Smith instantly. The other man had to be Max, "Don't worry," he said, "We're friends. We're going to get you out of here." As he grabbed a large bunch of keys from the table, Mr. Smith and Max began talking…

I told a friend of mine about the forgers. She said her father would help me, but I was captured before I could meet him.

I found the tunnel and planned to hand over the ear to David, my ex-boss. Since he was forced to sell out a year ago he's been investigating the goings-on at the fair and has collected evidence.

24

Their stories set Dick's brain racing. At last he was sure he was close to solving the case. If only he could have some time to think it all through logically, and find the right key to unlock the cell.

Meanwhile Mo was investigating the hall. She delved into some familiar packing cases and pulled out bundles of cash. "More forgeries I bet," Mo muttered, examining one carefully in the light. A sudden movement outside caught her eye. The three fairground villains were emerging from the trapdoor in the courtyard. "Here comes trouble," she yelled, dashing over to another window. She stared out and gasped. Dodgem and Tom were landing on one side of the island. From another window she spotted Sharkey and his mob.

"We've got to hide," Mo shouted. She spotted a rickety staircase leading up to a balcony. "Follow me Dick, and pick up those knives from the floor. I've got a plan."

All was quiet in the hall until suddenly one of the doors burst open and the fairground villains raced in. They froze as the door opposite was thrown open – in dashed Dodgem and Tom. Seconds later Sharkey and his gang appeared. The villains stared at each other in amazement.

"Now," Mo shouted. Before anyone below could move, she and Dick cut through the nets hanging from the balcony. The floor below was filled with struggling figures. Dick raced downstairs to check their catch.

He was in midstep when his nostrils suddenly twitched at the familiar smell of violets. Dick spotted Clare Voyant striding into the hall. Her earrings caught Dick's eye, triggering a distant memory in his mind.

Just then Dick missed the bottom step and landed with a bump. His head swam and so did his thoughts. Dick looked up and saw Carlotta standing over him. In a flash everything became clear. "I'm so glad you're safe," Carlotta breathed. "You've done a marvellous job."

"Correct," Dick replied, jumping to his feet. "Now I will explain the case of the fairground fires, and what's more I shall reveal the identity of the Scarab Society boss."

DON'T TURN THE PAGE YET. You now have all the information you need to solve the case of the fairground fires. Can you reveal the identity of the leader of the Scarab Society?

Dick Reveals All

Mo ran down to join Dick as he began. "At first, the case of the fairground fires appeared simple. The evidence against Dodgem seemed conclusive, but when Mo found Dodgem's glove at the Lido, it began to seem too neat. Would Dodgem really be so careless as to drop all those clues?"

"I didn't know what to make of it. But when I overheard Dodgem telling Tom that he had taken the plates to stop the forging operation, I began to wonder if Dodgem might be innocent. The proof was supplied by Max. The photos and the notes at Dodgem's hideout were not evidence against Dodgem, but were the evidence Dodgem had collected in his investigation of the fair. Max trusted Dodgem and was going to tell him about the tunnel, which is why he was kidnapped."

"But if Dodgem was innocent, who was framing him and why?" continued Dick. "The Scarab Society knew that Dodgem was on their trail, but thanks to Sharkey and his gang, they were so busy that they couldn't find him. That's where we came in. Dodgem was set up to look like a crook, then we were supposed to find Dodgem and lead the real villains to him. That's why we were hired by the leader of the Scarab Society . . . that's why we were hired by Carlotta Bottle!"

"This detective work has gone to your head," Carlotta said, smiling. "It's an interesting theory, but you have no proof."

"Who else could have told the three villains that we were coming to the fair?" Dick replied. "Your handwriting on the list of rides is identical to this scarab note. You also scribbled your telephone number on the torn cover of this book of matches . . . the very matches used to burn down the Wall of Death. You sabotaged your own business to frame your old enemy Dodgem. Finally, you are wearing the scarab ring."

"You think you're so clever," Carlotta snarled. "But you forgot one thing – my bodyguard. He bugged your phone and planted Dodgem's glove at the Lido. And he's right behind you. Hands up!"

Dick and Mo glumly did as they were ordered. Was this it? Was all their detective work going to end like this? As Carlotta's henchman stepped up to them, Mo spotted a flash of purple. An instant later, a crystal ball flew through the air, right on target.

The burly bodyguard collapsed to the floor. Carlotta grabbed for his gun, but Mo kicked it away. The pistol spun towards the net where a large, tattooed hand reached out and engulfed it. Mo remembered seeing the tattoo before, in a photo dropped by Carlotta's bodyguard. Now she recognized Tom as the undercover policeman in that photo.

Carlotta dashed for the door, just as police burst into the room. They handcuffed Carlotta and surrounded the net. Dodgem and Tom crawled out. "Well done, you two," Tom said to Dick and Mo. "We've wanted to nail this gang for ages. Thanks to you, the case is all wrapped up."

The villains were led away, but one thing was troubling Mo. Where did Clare Voyant fit in? "I worked out that you were our mystery caller from the scent of violets on the envelope you delivered," Dick said. "But I only realized your true identity when I recognized your earrings."

Mo gasped as Clare Voyant took off her hat and a wig to reveal . . . Viola Dodgem. After she explained her story, Dick turned to Mo. "All our hard work deserves a break. What do you say?"

"You must be joking," replied Mo. "Let's get back to the office. There may be another case for the Deckchair Detectives . . ."

I disguised myself to get a job at the fair and prove my father's innocence.

Detective Guide

This page will give you some help in solving the case. The numbers written here refer to the numbers inside the magnifying glasses found throughout the book.

1 There may be some useful information in the newspaper.
2 Take a good look at the evidence – it may come in handy.
3 Why is the security guard evesdropping outside the door?
4 What's suspicious about the whispering voice? It mentions Max, maybe it will make more sense later.
5 Look and listen carefully.
6 The message may not mean much now, but follow Dick's hunch and save it for later.
7 Flowers?
8 What are matches used for?
9 You're one step ahead of Dick and Mo here. Keep your eyes open.
10 Do you recognize the sinister stranger?
11 A perfect match?
12 Some of the information might be useful.
13 Read the documents carefully. They may contain useful information.
14 Have you seen any of these people before?
15 The symbol on the crates looks familiar.
16 Dick and Mo haven't got time to search the warehouse properly, but you should keep your eyes peeled.
17 Does this hand look familiar?
18 This conversation may be worth remembering.
19 Is Mo jumping to conclusions? Think back to the conversation which Dick overhead outside the deserted garage.
20 Dick may be right.
21 Does that ripped piece of paper match up with something you've seen before?
22 The villains seem to be expecting Dick and Mo.
23 Remember the voices Mo and Dick overheard outside the Hall of Mirrors.
24 Who is David?
25 Flowery smells again! Have you seen those earrings before?
26 A handy hint is just what you need here.

Did You Spot?

Now you've read the story and solved the mystery, check whether you spotted every clue. If you have difficulty reading this try holding this page in front of a mirror.

Carlotta was wearing the scarab ring from the very beginning.

The purple shadow glimpsed by Dick beside the Wall of Death on page 15 was none other than Clare Voyant, alias Viola Dodgem. This was where she discovered Carlotta's room match book.

Wherever she went, whether in disguise or not, Viola Dodgem always wore a flowery perfume smelling of violets. Viola means 'violet' in Latin.

Dick backed into Carlotta's henchman on page 18 as he was leaving Seaview Mansions. He was holding a screwdriver – probably used to bug the Deckchair Detectives' telephone.

Carlotta's henchman looked a bit like Dodgem – a red herring that may have confused you.

In the darkened room, not so far from Seaview Mansions (pages 20-21), the mystery speaker is wearing a scarab ring – this is Carlotta.

At the Lido, Carlotta's henchman dropped a glove ... a false clue to convince Dick and Mo that Dodgem had somehow nabbed Mr Smith. It's a pity he dropped another left-handed glove as the one on page 12 was also left-handed – Carlotta has made a mistake. The statue was also the work of Carlotta's henchman. In fact, Mr Smith was taken by Carlotta's three fairground villains.

The contents of the henchman's pockets were useful, but there were also a lot of red herrings. The screwdriver on page 26 was the one used by Carlotta's henchman to bug the Deckchair office. The Aliens in Albaraz is nonsense although the flickering lights were evidence of the Scarab Society's activities there. The newspaper article showing the crime leader's silhouette was way off mark. The henchman had Clare Voyant's card – perhaps she had recently read his palm.

The Scarab Society probably used the fairground tunnel from Albaraz in their notorious breakout from the Albaraz jail (as mentioned in the Deckchair Document on page 26).

Did you notice Steve Same (see document on page 27) in the picture on page 29?

If you wondered what Dodgem was doing at the warehouse, he was gathering vital evidence against the Scarab Society's activities. You can see him taking the forging plate on page 30.

Tom is an undercover police officer. You can see the tattoo on his right hand on the photo on page 26.

Viola knew about the Scarab Society's activities from her father. She was the mystery caller on page 19. Viola hoped Dick and Mo would help but couldn't afford to blow her cover at this point.

MURDER
UNLIMITED

Emma Fischel

Illustrated by Ann Johns

Designed by
Paul Greenleaf and Ann Johns

Contents

An Invitation

A letter! Eagerly, Al ripped open the envelope that had just dropped onto the mat. The handwriting seemed vaguely familiar, but whose was it?

Some pieces of paper fell out and she picked them up. It's from Uncle Russ, she thought. But it's not my birthday. Why else would he write to me?

Puzzled, Al began to read. It took quite some time but when she had finished, she went to see her friend Dan. "Take a look at this," she said, handing him the envelope . . .

What is it, Al?

Read it and see. Let's go!

July 1

Captain Russ T. Rowlocks
Prancing Prawn
Loukaniki Bay
Mythika

My dearest niece Alyssum

How does a week aboard the Prancing Prawn sound? My usual deck crew are away on an Amphibian Recognition course in the first week of August. Would you and a friend stand in for them? The boat has been chartered by Jolyon Scrupulous, some kind of inventor chappie. Perhaps you have heard of him. He's made himself a small fortune by all accounts. (The booking was strictly secret, but no one seemed interested anyway when I mentioned it in Queezy-Sleezies' cafe a couple of weeks ago.)

I have enclosed my brand new brochure about Prancing Prawn Tours. I'm rather proud of it. (Also enclosed is a photo of the boat.) The people in the brochure photo with me are the other crew members. Max is a dear fellow but temperamental - he's been with me for years. Dida appeared out of the blue about a week ago - an uncanny stroke of luck, almost as if she knew I needed her before I did!

Anyway, I hope you can come. There are daily flights from Delaise airport direct to Loukaniki.

Affectionately, Uncle Russ

PRANCING PRAWN TOURS

Hop aboard the Prancing Prawn, the ultimate in comfort and safety! Available for charter from Loukaniki by parties of up to twelve.

- Spacious accommodation, splendid food, sparkling entertainment
- Two sun decks, two lounges, large dining room
- Powerful engine, dinghy with outboard motor, up-to-the-minute radio equipment

Book early to avoid disappointment! Children under one foot go free! Special rates for the over-80's!

So sit back and let us do the wor...

With your captain:

- Diamond de'Ath, your friendly hostess. Dida will cater to your every whim. Anything you can think of, she can organize!
- Max Kaloris, wonder chef! Max will tempt your palate daily. Just wait until you taste his pillaka fillets!

...e entertained by performers on the streets of Pathos.

The enchanted world of Mythika and its islands awaits you! Drop anchor in the coastal bays or hop from island to island. The choice is yours!

A warm and friendly people are waiting to bid you hello!

On the Waterfront

T he morning sun shimmered in a cloudless sky. The heat was already stifling. Al and Dan walked slowly along the waterfront, squinting in the bright early light. In front of them the Fatimian Sea stretched away smooth and still. Hardly a ripple disturbed its surface.

Clutching the photo her uncle had sent, Al looked around for the boat. The tangy smell of salt filled the air. A seagull swooped over their heads. Uttering a mournful cry, it turned and flew out to sea. Soon it was just a tiny speck on the horizon.

A faint breath of wind ruffled the water. Then they saw it – there, bobbing gently at anchor out in the bay, was the Prancing Prawn. Al and Dan stared hard at the boat. This would be their first time at sea, so who could tell what the week might hold in store...

Squalls be a'brewing far out at sea.

Suddenly, Al felt a hand tap her shoulder. She spun around and gasped. Who was this mysterious stranger who stood before her? He began to speak, in low and urgent tones.

When the morning sun blazes from an aquamarine sky, perilous times lie ahead.

Before the tide turns for a fifth time, storm clouds will gather on the horizon.

Mark my words well, young strangers. Danger lies waiting for those who put to sea.

Would he never stop? The stranger stared at them with piercing eyes, blue as the Fatimian Sea, while the prophecies of doom issued from his sun-blistered lips.

Then his face turned pale. He clutched Al's arm and pointed a bony finger at the photo she held in her hand. Once more, he spoke. "There's something bad out there. The birds don't fly near that boat. And the birds always know."

With that, the stranger hurried away, but far down the road he stopped and called back over his shoulder. "Be wary, be watchful – and look out for the fifth turn of the tide." Then he disappeared from view.

For a moment, Al and Dan stood, bemused. But there was no time to wonder. Across the bay came a booming voice. "Ahoy there, landlubbers. Come aboard!"

Waving at them from the deck of the Prancing Prawn was a portly figure dressed in white and blue. And out in the bay a small boat chugged steadily to meet them.

Dida is on her way!

The Plain Brown Envelope

The Captain gave Al a hearty kiss and Dan a firm handshake as they clambered on deck. "Welcome aboard," he beamed. Meanwhile, Dida bustled busily away.

Call me Uncle Russ too, Dan!

"We've got a packed week ahead," the Captain continued. "So I've cobbled together a few things you might find it useful to know."

With that, he handed them a plain brown envelope, then left. Al and Dan sat down and began to sift through the contents.

PASSENGERS

Jolyon Scrupulous, millionaire inventor and businessman. Mona Lott, his wife, famous Hollywood actress. Star of box office smash Eek! Due to start filming sequel on return from cruise. Accompanied by Jolyon Junior (JJ), their son.

Cliff Hanger, assistant to Scrupulous for the last five months. Before that was a research scientist studying medical uses for reptile venom.

Rula Margin, nanny to JJ for this trip only. Last-minute replacement for regular nanny who was taken ill. Oldest of nine children brought up in lighthouse on Hazard Rock. Used to be a nurse.

Dermot Dither, along as my guest. Old school friend. Shared a tambour Music and Movement cr and been friends ever sinc Inclined to be bossy.

CREW

Max Kaloris, chef. Navigator before turned to cookery. Mythikan, but spent much of childhood overseas. Has been jittery and absent-minded lately.

Diamond (Dida) de'Ath, responsible for passenger care. Seems reluctant to talk about herself, but left last job just over four months ago. Has spent time since on travel.

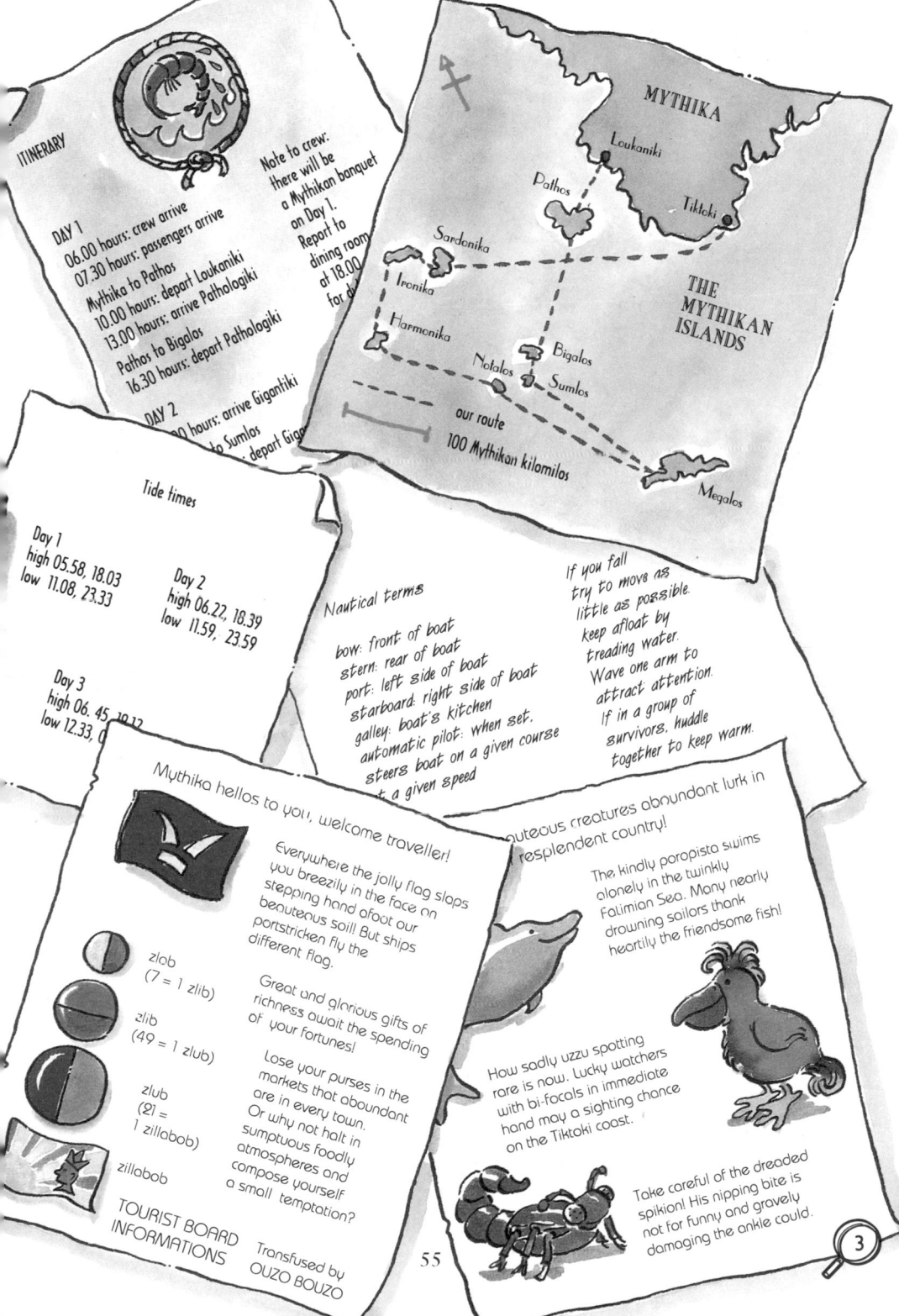

ITINERARY

DAY 1
06.00 hours: crew arrive
07.30 hours: passengers arrive

Mythika to Pathos
10.00 hours: depart Loukaniki
13.00 hours: arrive Pathologiki

Pathos to Bigalos
16.30 hours: depart Pathologiki

DAY 2
0.00 hours: arrive Gigantiki
to Sumlos
depart Giga

Note to crew:
there will be
a Mythikan banquet
on Day 1.
Report to
dining room
at 18.00
for d

MYTHIKA

Loukaniki

Pathos

Tiktoki

Sardonika

Ironika

THE
MYTHIKAN
ISLANDS

Harmonika

Notalos   Bigalos
Sumlos

our route
100 Mythikan kilomilos

Megalos

Tide times

Day 1
high 05.58, 18.03
low 11.08, 23.33

Day 2
high 06.22, 18.39
low 11.59, 23.59

Day 3
high 06. 45, 19.12
low 12.33, 0

Nautical terms

bow: front of boat
stern: rear of boat
port: left side of boat
starboard: right side of boat
galley: boat's kitchen
automatic pilot: when set,
steers boat on a given course
t a given speed

If you fall
try to move as
little as possible.
keep afloat by
treading water.
Wave one arm to
attract attention.
If in a group of
survivors, huddle
together to keep warm.

Mythika hellos to you, welcome traveller!

Everywhere the jolly flag slaps
you breezily in the face on
stepping hand afoot our
beauteous soil! But ships
portstricken fly the
different flag.

Great and glorious gifts of
richness await the spending
of your fortunes!

Lose your purses in the
markets that aboundant
are in every town.
Or why not halt in
sumptuous foodly
atmospheres and
compose yourself
a small temptation?

zlob
(7 = 1 zlib)

zlib
(49 = 1 zlub)

zlub
(21 =
1 zillabob)

zillabob

TOURIST BOARD
INFORMATIONS

Transfused by
OUZO BOUZO

guteous creatures abundant lurk in
resplendent country!

The kindly poropista swims
alonely in the twinkly
Falimian Sea. Many nearly
drowning sailors thank
heartily the friendsome fish!

How sadly uzzu spotting
rare is now. Lucky watchers
with bi-focals in immediate
hand may a sighting chance
on the Tiktoki coast.

Take careful of the dreaded
spikion! His nipping bite is
not for funny and gravely
damaging the ankle could.

3

All Aboard!

The roar of a powerboat approaching made Al and Dan look up from their reading. Then the engine cut out and, through the silence, a voice bellowed out. "Ahoy there, beam us up!"

Jolyon Scrupulous had arrived! He stepped onto the deck, closely followed by his wife and small son. Bringing up the rear was Dermot Dither, struggling with a vast quantity of luggage.

The mega-millionaire and ruthless man of business removed a cigar from between his fat pink lips. "Who's in charge of this floating bathtub?" he asked, as he flicked the soggy stub overboard.

 The Captain had just launched into a stiff speech of welcome when a sudden gust of wind took them all by surprise. It blew Dida's hat off, and she leaped to retrieve it. Unfortunately, so did Dither. With a loud crack their heads collided. Irritated by this interruption, the Captain continued. "We leave at ten prompt," he barked. He turned to Al and Dan. "The last provisions will arrive soon. If you need me, I shall be studying my charts." With that, he left.

Jolyon Scrupulous turned to face Dida. "Where's my room?" he demanded, clutching his mobile phone. "I've got calls to make." Dida ushered the new arrivals off to the stairs, leaving Al and Dan alone.

They heard the putt-putt of an ancient engine, followed by a thud as the the Prancing Prawn was rammed in the side by a small boat.

Al and Dan rushed to the rails and looked over the side. The occupants of the boat below seemed to be having some difficulty. A lanky figure dangled half-in and half-out of the water and, wedged awkwardly in the bottom of the boat, was a large pink shape. This must be Cliff Hanger and Rula Margin arriving!

Once on deck the ungainly pair went right away to see Jolyon Scrupulous. Then the stores began to arrive. Two hours later, nearly all the provisions were aboard – but not quite everything...

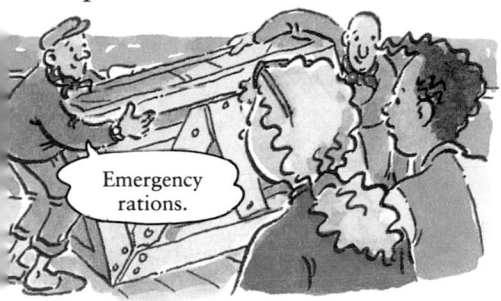

A couple of smiling characters heaved a huge crate aboard. "We'll secure it nice and tight, then be off," said the one with the hat.

Al rubbed her eyes. Had the one with the hat just winked at the other, or was he squinting in the strong morning light?

At exactly ten the Captain appeared. "Up anchor!" he bellowed, and Al and Dan sprang swiftly into action.

The heavy vibration of the engine throbbed through the boat. Then the Prancing Prawn slewed around and headed slowly out to sea.

But unknown to anyone aboard, someone was watching them leave. Perched high on a hilltop above the town, the mysterious stranger gazed out across the bay.

The eerie cries of the birds that circled around him floated out over the shimmering Fatimian Sea. His piercing blue eyes followed the slow path of the old boat to the distant horizon and, as he watched, was he shaking his head in despair?

Cabin Crew

Al and Dan watched the shoreline gradually fade until it disappeared completely. Then the Prancing Prawn was alone, chugging full steam ahead for the distant island of Pathos. Birds flew high above the sparkling blue sea, but not one flew near the boat.

Once away from the shelter of the land, a stiff breeze whipped salt spray into their faces. Small waves slapped against the hull of the boat. Dan shivered. "Let's find our bunks," he said, and they headed below to look at the boat plan.

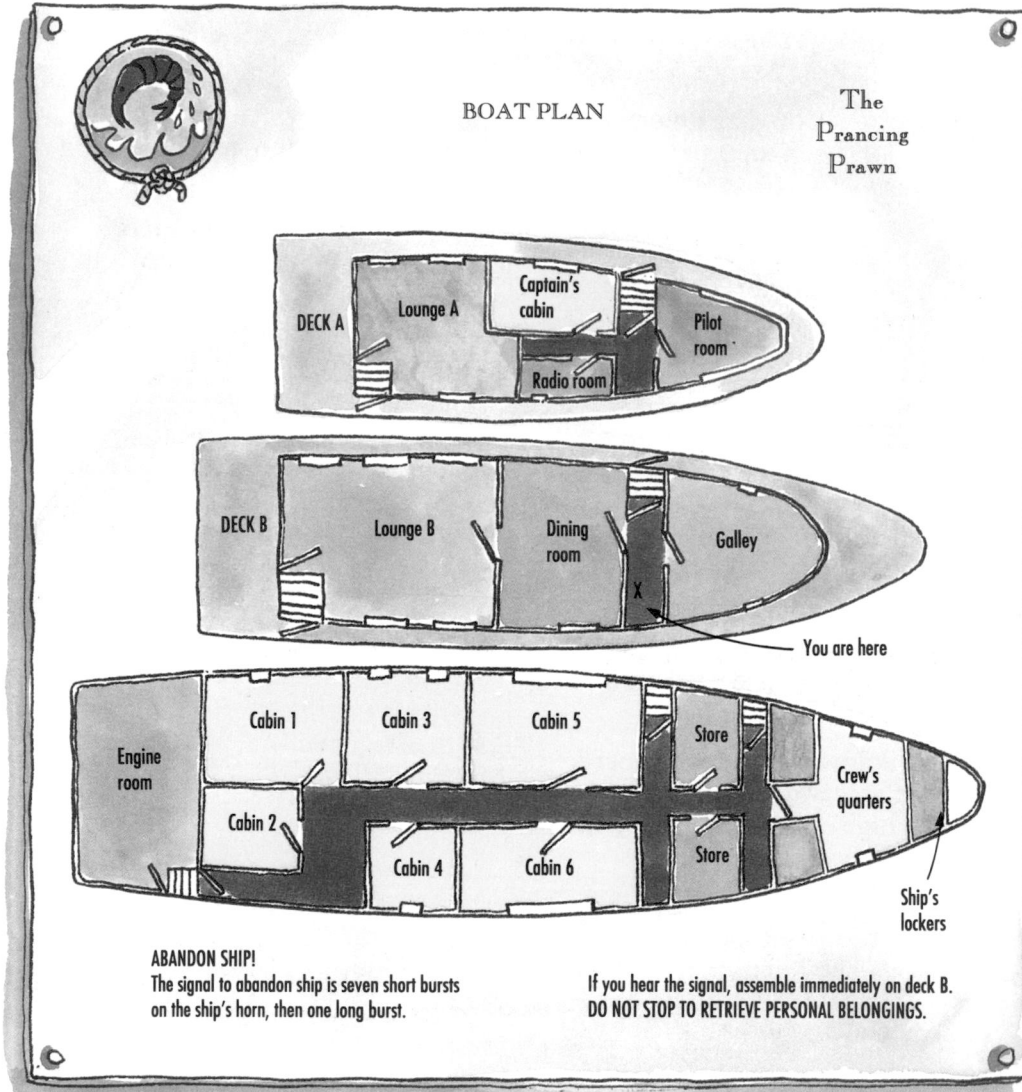

BOAT PLAN

The Prancing Prawn

DECK A — Lounge A · Captain's cabin · Radio room · Pilot room

DECK B — Lounge B · Dining room · Galley

X — You are here

Engine room · Cabin 1 · Cabin 3 · Cabin 5 · Store · Crew's quarters · Cabin 2 · Cabin 4 · Cabin 6 · Store · Ship's lockers

ABANDON SHIP!
The signal to abandon ship is seven short bursts on the ship's horn, then one long burst.

If you hear the signal, assemble immediately on deck B.
DO NOT STOP TO RETRIEVE PERSONAL BELONGINGS.

Dan opened the door to the crew's quarters and inched inside. Al squeezed in behind him. It certainly seemed snug.

Just as they wedged the last of their luggage into the narrow drawers under the bottom bunk, a familiar voice floated in through the open porthole. "Crew on deck!"

The Captain had a long list of chores for the day. "You can start with the portholes," he beamed. "Shouldn't take long once you get into the swing of it."

They quickly realized what the Captain meant. Cleaning some of the portholes proved to be a precarious task...

Soon Dan was dangling from a swinging wooden seat just a few feet above the water. Some job, he thought, as he scrubbed wearily at the glass. This would be his tenth porthole.

He stopped for a moment to rest his aching arms and peered idly into the cabin. Some people do choose to take strange things on a cruise, he mused.

Half an hour later, the final porthole was sparklingly clean. But there was no time to rest. Some energetic deck swabbing lay ahead of them.

Al sloshed soapy water over the deck, while Dan scrubbed at the wooden planks. The sounds of conversation drifted down the boat. A booming voice with a hearty laugh seemed to be coming from the radio room.

Ten minutes later, the Captain stamped up to them. He looked red-faced and very angry indeed.

A Sudden Move

The Captain started to speak in a grumbling voice. "This trip is turning out to be a real headache. First a crate appears out of the blue, cluttering up the deck. No one warned *me*! And the next thing I know, Mr. Extremely Scrupulous tells Dida he wants to move. He claims he doesn't like cabin 6. Ridiculous!"

"So," the Captain continued, with an exasperated sigh, "I want you to move some luggage. I suggest that we move Rula out of cabin 5 to cabin 6, and then our fussy friend into cabin 5."

Leaving the Captain still complaining, Al and Dan headed for cabin 5. Rula's bags lay bulging on the floor. Scooping up one each, Al and Dan staggered to the door. Then Dan stumbled and the bag he was carrying flew out of his hand. It hit the floor. With a loud click, the lid flew up and all the contents spilled out.

UU Newsletter

STOP PRESS!!!
Our breeding site at Happy Days is under threat.

Donations urgent stop developers! now!

PPY DAYS HIDEAWAY!
animals and birds roam free and appy in a natural setting. Sample the delights of a get-away-from-it-all week in one of our camouflaged chalets.

Our newest little visitor, the uzzu. Once found all over the globe, this charming little bird is now native only to Mythika. But, thanks to Uzzus Unite, it will soon have a special breeding site in the Happy Days grounds!

Located just outside the quiet coastal village of Tiktoki, the Happy Days Hideaway will give you a break to remember. "Thank you, Happy Days!" writes RM of Loukaniki. "You made my summer. I'll be back!"

Over there! Two hikers spot a nesting uzzu.

UZZU SPOTTER'S HANDBOOK

PROTECT OUR UZZUS!

UZZUS UNITE! Member: 27

Al and Dan could hardly believe their eyes. A most peculiar assortment of things littered the floor.

Dan bundled everything back in the case and shut the lid, then Al opened the door. Outside, two people were skulking in the corridor, and they were deep in conversation.

Make no mistake, Rula... going to pay...

Bath every night... five until five-thirty... never varies!

Al and Dan couldn't help overhearing a few snippets of what Cliff and Rula were saying. It seemed to be a very odd discussion indeed.

Then Cliff looked up and saw them. He gave a jump. Nervously, he took out a grubby cotton handkerchief and blew his nose on it noisily.

"Just getting acquainted," tittered Rula. "After all, we are going to be shipmates for quite a while."

Dan was puzzled. From what they had heard it seemed clear that Rula and Cliff were already well acquainted. So why would Rula lie? Before he could wonder any more, the sound of a high-pitched, angry voice drifted out into the corridor. It was coming from inside cabin 6.

This is the last straw. This time you've gone too far!

About time!

How nice!

Outside cabin 6, Al hesitated, then she lifted her hand and rapped on the door. Nervously, she pushed it open. Not everyone inside the cabin seemed entirely happy. "Our luggage is on the bed over there," snapped Jolyon Scrupulous. "Move it now!"

Al and Dan hurried across the room. All of a sudden, there was a furious noise from outside – the noise of feet pounding along the corridor at great speed. Then the cabin door burst open.

Everyone inside the room recoiled in horror. In front of them was a wild-eyed figure, maddened with rage. And in his hand he brandished a very sharp bread knife...

The Missing Melons

Someone aboard this boat is a thief!

This must be Max Kaloris! Puce with rage, he glared around cabin 6. "My entire stock of melons – stolen!" he bellowed, slicing the bread knife through the air. Then he turned to Jolyon Scrupulous. "And by one of your party!" he hissed.

"They were there at ten, ripened to perfection," elaborated the Mythikan master chef. "But by noon, there they were, gone! Wait until I find the culprit...!" With that, he flounced out of the room and slammed the door. A folded piece of paper fluttered to the floor behind him.

For a moment everyone stood stunned. Then Al heaved a couple of suitcases off the bed. "Let's go," she said to Dan, picking up the piece of paper by the door on her way out.

At last the move was completed. Leaving the new occupants of cabins 5 and 6 to settle in, Al and Dan went up on deck.

Look. Melon seeds!

They stared down at their feet. A sticky trail of melon juice, not yet dried by the sun, dribbled along deck A. Every so often, clumps of seeds lay splattered on the varnished wooden planks. Then the trail stopped. But behind the boat, a line of melon rinds bobbed about in the choppy wake left by the Prancing Prawn.

"Who on earth would steal the melons?" asked Al, confused. Before Dan could reply a deafening crash echoed around the boat, followed by a muffled scream and strange thumping, groaning noises...

A Narrow Escape

Al and Dan pounded down the stairs. The sound of running feet came from all directions. It seemed everyone had heard the noise. Dither overtook them in the corridor. "I'll deal with this. Stand back," he ordered, flinging open the door to cabin 6.

Just then, the ship's horn sounded. With a shudder, the engine began to slow down. They were arriving at Pathos.

Surprises on Shore

The Prancing Prawn chugged into the port. Dither stayed below to comfort a shaken Rula, while everyone else rushed on deck. It was market day and the busy waterfront was bustling with life.

Clutching a long shopping list, Al and Dan hurried ashore and into the thick of the market. The main street was packed with stalls groaning under the weight of piles of exotic food.

At two o'clock, hot, weary and hungry, they bought a snack. Al spent two zlob on a slice of Pathosian snibblebite, while Dan chose a juicy malingo fruit. Outside the door of the Mythikan National Bank they started to eat, then suddenly they heard a great commotion.

Al and Dan watched in amazement as a figure hurtled out of the bank door, propelled by the heavy hand of a burly security guard. It was Cliff! He lay on the dusty street, shouting.

The security guard remained unmoved. "Boss's new rule. No credit and no time to pay," she growled.

Cliff picked himself up. He didn't notice Al or Dan. "I'll get the money, you'll see," he muttered, turning to go. "I'll just have to act faster than planned."

What was all that about? Confused, Al and Dan made their way to Ouzo the Outfitters. They each had four zlub to spend on a Mythikan national costume for the evening's banquet.

It was difficult to concentrate on the suggestions of the helpful shop assistant. A hissing voice was filtering through the patterned curtain of the changing room. And from what they could hear, the owner of the voice sounded furious about something.

At last the bitter outburst came to a halt and, with a swish of the curtain, who should come out but Mona! Tight-lipped, she swirled out of the shop in a cloud of strong perfume.

After that, Al and Dan were hardly aware of what outfits they chose. They left the shop with two brightly wrapped bundles.

They made their way back to the Prancing Prawn. By four-thirty, the boat was on its way to Bigalos and, with some relief, Al and Dan headed below deck to their cabin.

"What a peculiar day!" said Dan, collapsing in an exhausted heap on the bottom bunk.

"Mmm," agreed Al with a groan. "And it's not over yet." She shifted uncomfortably on the hard bunk. Something rustled in her back pocket and she jumped up. Of course! She had forgotten all about the piece of paper Max had dropped earlier.

She fished it out of her pocket, unfolded it and tried to smooth out the crumples. It was a magazine article. Something in it caught her eye...

STAR GAZING

Juster Snoop profiles Jolyon Scrupulous, the man with the millions!

"Unpopular – me? Of course! I've never cared about being liked. That's why I'm rich!" Jolyon Scrupulous, millionaire inventor now turned businessman, was speaking by the pool of his luxury villa in Tiktoki. "I've built my fortune by inventing useless things," he chortled. "Then I persuade people that they need them!"

We were interrupted by shouts from behind the high-security gates. Protesters from a local nature sanctuary were out in force. Jolyon plans to build a leisure centre that will cut through the sanctuary and halt proposals for an uzzu haven. After a small scuffle the protesters were ejected.

Unperturbed, Jolyon continued our interview. "In my position you can't afford to mind what people

> **"I've never cared about being liked. That's why I'm rich!"**

think of you," he said. But did he gaze wistfully for a moment at his little son splashing in the pool?

Business buying

Over the last three years, Jolyon's inventions have made him millions. Now he is expanding his horizons. In a shock move nearly five months ago, he bought up the Tuffaware All-Weather Anorak chain. That was swiftly followed by the acquisition of the Mythikan National Bank. Jolyon's methods have caused strong murmurs of disapproval in the business community. He plans a change in loan policy at Mythikan National that will leave thousands of customers losers, leading some to call him the most ruthless business brain of the decade.

▼ Family man Jolyon likes nothing better than the rare opportunity to relax at home.

▲ Jolyon stays in shape with a brisk swim each morning – in between business deals!

▲ Jolyon and his tragic former partner on the way to discuss the Tuffaware take-over bid.

Surprise marriage

After a whirlwind courtship two years ago, Jolyon married Hollywood film star Mona Lott. "He just swept me off my feet," said Mona after the secret wedding in Las Tingbliss.

Friends of the star had long expected that she would marry her producer Sven Gayley, who some credit with her success. Their stormy relationship and massive public arguments had led many to suspect a romance between the pair but, instead, they settled recently for a ten-year contract.

Tragic accident

"It was the biggest shock of my life!" said Jolyon, talking about the recent sad disappearance of his business partner. Best known as the former child-star impressionist Teeny Dimple, his partner

> **"It was the biggest shock of my life!"**

disappeared in mysterious circumstances in March, missing presumed drowned.

One source believes Jolyon's partner was very disturbed by the move into take-overs, and may even have been collecting information about fraudulent business deals.

Scoop! We can exclusively reveal that Mona and Jolyon have chartered a Loukanikian cruiser in August. Look out Mythikans!

Rags to riches

The Scrupulous story began when the poor boy from Lessenless County gained an early scholarship to Ablution College, famous throughout the world for its academic excellence. There his brilliant mind

"Scrupulous used to pick on me!"

shone through, although he was not popular and gained a reputation as something of a bully.

One old classmate claims he lived in daily fear: "Scrupulous used to pick on me and pinch my pastry cutter, just because I liked to spend weekends sticking recipes in my scrapbook."

Career changes

On leaving school, Jolyon dabbled in many things. As a student biochemist he spent a year in isolated and treacherous conditions up the Intrepid river studying the plant and animal life. Then he turned to banking, followed by a spell on an oil tanker. After that came SLIME, and the foundation of the whole Scrupulous empire . . .

▲ A rare photo of Jolyon the schoolboy, having fun with his classmates.

◀ As a student, living rough up the wild Intrepid river.

SLIME

SLIME was the brainchild of Jolyon Scrupulous and his former business partner. Together they created a dynamic new computer program that rocked the world and led them to fame and fortune. Launched onto the market with a massive billboard campaign reproduced below, the eager public couldn't buy it fast enough. People queued in the streets to get their hands on it. Shops sold out as fast as new stocks arrived. Copies were exchanging hands for fantastic sums. Then the government stepped in and the product was banned. But it had already made Jolyon millions.

SLIME

Supersonic Lies Incorporating Mega Excuses

Lie your way out of any tricky situation!

Haven't done your homework?
Late for work again?
Forgot to go to your wedding?
Pan-fried your best friend?

Just tap in your problem,
SLIME *will give you the solution!*
Excuses for every occasion!

 SLIME changed my life! Miss O Dear, Pankhurst Prison

 Brilliant! I use it every day! Freckles, Swotville

 Thank you, SLIME! Teacher, Truanting College

Chef's Special

With a loud dong, the ship's clock struck six. "Quick!" said Dan, putting down the magazine article. "The Mythikan banquet!" Then he shot off in the direction of the stairs.

Strange smells were wafting out of the galley as they reached the dining room. Inside, Dida was tapping her foot impatiently.

Dida started issuing instructions thick and fast.

So that's four knives, three forks, two spoons...

But first of all...

!*!

Time galloped by.

At last Dan made the final fold.

Then Max announced the meal.

I give you a feast to tantalize your taste buds!

A Mythikan Evening

MENU
Gherkori Fritters
* * *
Kluk-Klukis
Deep-sea Ziggazagga
* * *
Snibblebite
Baked Baliki

Guests at Mythikan feasts are required to don paper hats after the fish course.

Baked baliki is eaten on festive occasions. Each guest receives a portion bearing a flag. On the flag is a motto appropriate to the guest.

Dither Takes Charge

A stunned silence greeted Dither's statement. Jolyon Scrupulous was the first to recover. "Nonsense," he said impatiently. "A case of mild food poisoning, that's all. Anyway, who are you to take charge?" Dither glared, then fumbled around in his pocket...

Dermot Dither
Special Agent

13.10.91

Dither
of the Yard!

Dither flourished his ID card importantly. "I came here in a civilian capacity," he said. "But now it seems my professional skills are needed."

Shrewdly, he scrutinized the group in front of him. "We appear to have a cold-blooded attempt at poisoning. And is it coincidence that a deadly snake was on the loose earlier? I think not!"

The Captain was in some distress. "I can't believe this could happen," he muttered. "I run a tight ship. What should I do?"

"Rowlocks," said Dither, patting his old friend kindly on the shoulder. "I suggest you start by fetching Kaloris. There are a few questions he needs to answer."

It is a crime to do this to my baked balikis! And you accuse me – me! I loved that dish!

Three minutes later Max appeared. He seemed upset. Dither spoke with authority. "Calm down," he ordered. "No one is accusing you of anything – yet."

"It is likely that the poison was added in the galley," Dither continued. "But who had the opportunity? Max, of course, but did he leave the galley at any point, I wonder? Anyone else could have done it then."

"At six o'clock I went to talk to the Captain," said Max, sniffling. "I had just made the balikis. I left them on a tray, ready for baking later. It was six thirty-five when I returned."

Dither's eyes moved slowly over face after face. "In that case, I must ask each of you to account for your movements between six o'clock and the evening meal," he said solemnly.

There was a buzz of outrage. Then the Captain spoke. "Surely you can't mean to include Mona or Rula," he objected gallantly. "They were the victims!"

"Were they? Victims of what? After all, neither attempt actually worked," said Dither. "No, until we know what we are dealing with – and why – no one can be excluded." Before anyone could raise more objections, he continued. "Something strange is going on aboard this boat. We need to find out what before anything worse happens!"

> I was in my cabin. I read two chapters of the latest novel by B. A. Crook.

> I was in the pilot room. Max came in at four minutes past six. He stayed about half an hour.

> I was in the dining room all the time. I was busy with the banquet. I didn't notice anyone go past the window.

> I don't seem to remember. Let me see. I'm not sure... I had a cup of tea, then I think I must have fallen asleep.

> I was in the bath, playing with a few ideas. I plan to shake the world of packaging with my new zippered milk carton very soon.

> I was catching up on some paperwork in my cabin. I heard no one and I never left the room.

> I took Jolyon Junior around the deck. I saw nobody. It was getting quite dark.

Reluctantly, one by one they disclosed their whereabouts. Then again Dither spoke, in a voice loaded with warning. "Ladies and gentlemen, I suggest we take the quickest possible route to land. Until then, I urge you all to tread very carefully indeed. Exercise the utmost caution. Go to your cabins and lock the doors. Speak to no one until we arrive in port, or who can tell who might be the next victim!"

What Next?

There was an uneasy silence after Dither's words. Then the Captain spoke. "We'll turn back to Pathos. With the wind and tide against us, I estimate it will take seven hours. But going on to Bigalos would take much longer." Hurriedly, he left.

Soon the frightened group made their way to the cabin deck. Doors slammed and keys turned, then Dither stationed himself on guard.

Inside the crew's quarters, Al got out her brand-new notepad and pen set. She began to write...

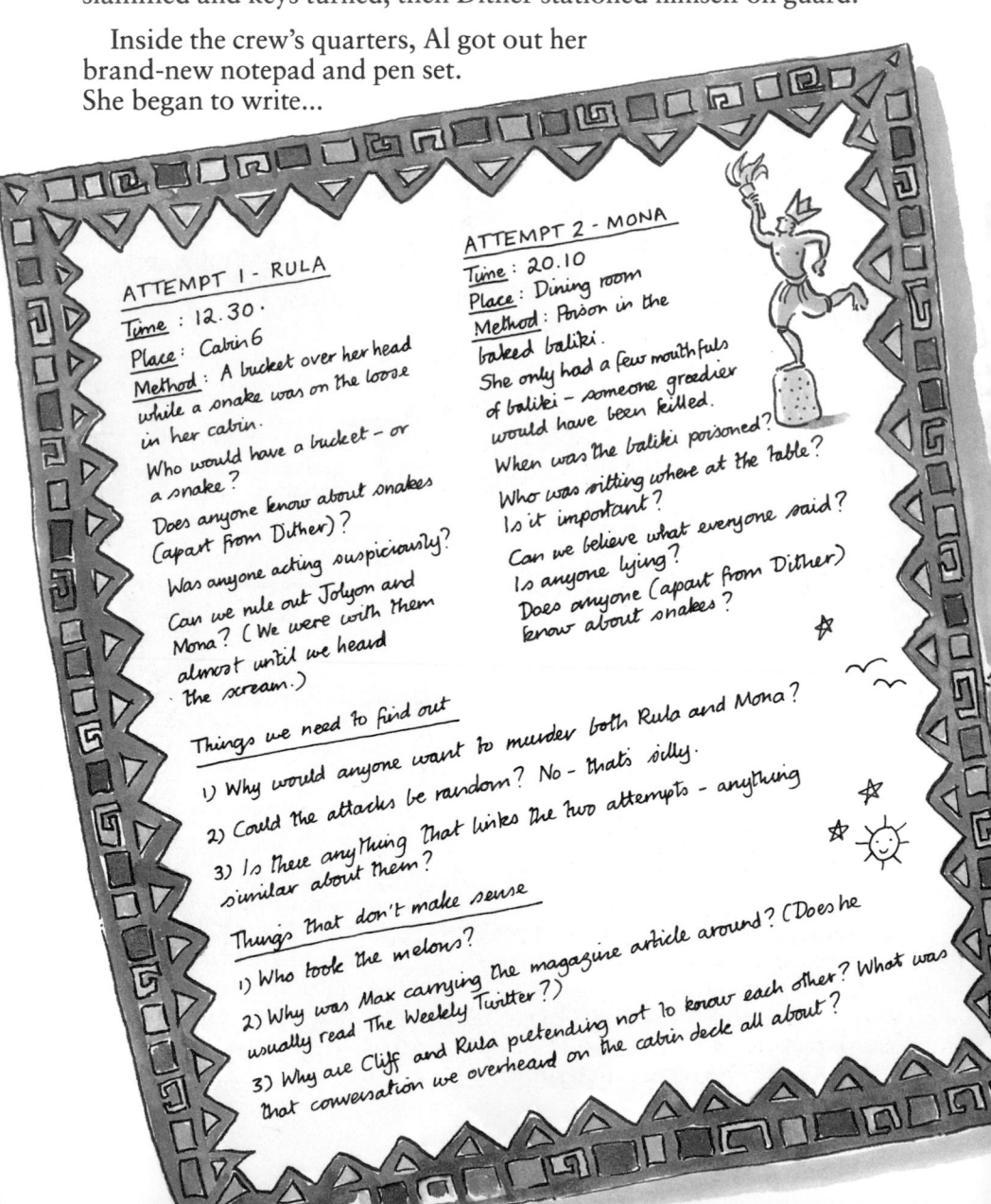

ATTEMPT 1 - RULA

Time : 12.30.
Place : Cabin 6
Method : A bucket over her head while a snake was on the loose in her cabin.

Who would have a bucket - or a snake?

Does anyone know about snakes (apart from Dither)?

Was anyone acting suspiciously?

Can we rule out Jolyon and Mona? (We were with them almost until we heard the scream.)

ATTEMPT 2 - MONA

Time : 20.10
Place : Dining room
Method : Poison in the baked baliki.
She only had a few mouthfuls of baliki - someone greedier would have been killed.

When was the baliki poisoned?

Who was sitting where at the table? Is it important?

Can we believe what everyone said? Is anyone lying?

Does anyone (apart from Dither) know about snakes?

Things we need to find out

1) Why would anyone want to murder both Rula and Mona?

2) Could the attacks be random? No - that's silly.

3) Is there anything that links the two attempts - anything similar about them?

Things that don't make sense

1) Who took the melons?

2) Why was Max carrying the magazine article around? (Does he usually read The Weekly Twitter?)

3) Why are Cliff and Rula pretending not to know each other? What was that conversation we overheard on the cabin deck all about?

RULA

Victim. Why?
What about her luggage?
Has been to Happy Days
Hideaway in Tiktoki. Is
this important?

MONA

Victim. Why?
What about her conversation
in Ouzo the Outfitters? Who
was she speaking to?
Suspiciously unable to
remember what she was
doing between six and the
meal. Unable or unwilling?

MAX

Easy for him to poison the
baliki – but for what
motive? Too obvious?

UNCLE RUSS AND DITHER

Above suspicion?

What else do we know about anyone?
Is there anything we have overlooked?

CLIFF

Was he in his cabin when
he said he was?
What about that strange
scene outside the
Mythikan National Bank?

DIDA

Was she in the dining
room all the time
between six and the
meal? Would we have
noticed if she had
left (we were very
busy)?

SEND MUM
POSTCARD

JOLYON SCRUPULOUS

Why did he change cabins?
Should we read the
magazine article again?

Buy Spiodge a present

"That wasn't much help," sighed
Al as she put the lid back on the pen.

Dan drummed his heels nervously on the floor. Someone aboard was
the villainous would-be killer. But who? And would they get safely to port
before he or she struck again?

Al yawned. "I can't think any more," she said. "Let's set the alarm for
four. We should be nearly at Pathos by then." But little did she know,
things weren't going to go quite according to plan...

Sabotage!

Rrrring! It was four o'clock. Blearily, Al and Dan stumbled out onto the chilly deck. Pale fingers of light were just streaking the sky. Surely there should be some sign of Pathos by now? But all they could see was choppy grey sea in all directions.

"What was that noise?" said Al suddenly. "I think it came from one of the cabins!" They rushed below decks and found Dither inching the engine room door open. Strange moaning sounds were coming from inside. "Leave this to me," hissed Dither.

> Oooourrrgh!

"Captain Rowlocks!"
"My dear chap!"
"What happened, Uncle Russ?"

Shocked, they all spoke at once. At the foot of the stairs, the Captain lay slumped. "I went to turn the boat around," he groaned. "But everything was jammed. Calamity! I hurried down here to sort things out..."

The light wouldn't work.

Then I heard a noise.

> CRRRRK!

Fearlessly, I called out.

> H-h-halloooo?

Suddenly I saw something. I spun around.

> Who's there?

I saw the frozen chicken too late!

That's all I remember.

"I must have been knocked out cold," concluded the Captain. "The next thing I knew, I was lying where you found me."

"Impossible!" blustered Dither. "Why, I was on watch the whole time. Who could have passed me?"

"No idea," said the Captain, struggling to stand up. He blew his nose loudly. "First a roving reptile, then poison, now sabotage! Never, in all my years at sea – "

"Let's radio for help," interrupted Dither decisively. Al, Dan and the Captain followed him along the corridor. There was no noise from any of the cabins. Everyone seemed to be sleeping very soundly.

Inside the radio room, a shock lay in store...

"Things are looking grim," said Dither gravely. He clutched onto a table as he spoke. The old boat was beginning to roll more and more in the increasing swell. Outside, storm clouds were gathering in a darkening sky. "We can't change course," he continued. "We can't change speed, and we can't radio for help!"

The Captain had been doing some calculations. He spoke heavily. "It appears that we are locked on course for Megalos. And that's twenty-four hours away!"

Man Overboard

Twenty-four hours! This was a new and dangerous development. The only course of safety now was to stick together. On Dither's orders, Al and Dan hurried to wake everyone and bring them to lounge B.

"First murder, now sabotage. What on – oof!" said Al, cannoning into Dan. He had stopped abruptly, halfway down the stairs.

"Did you hear something?" he asked, starting to run. "Like a faint cry?"

"Not again!" said Al. She struggled to keep up as she pounded along in his footsteps.

"It's coming from over the side!" said Dan, racing along deck B.

"Impossible!" said Al in disbelief.

Then she saw the mega-magnate – and what a sight he made. Pink-faced and grunting, he dangled from the flagpole, saved from a watery grave only by the grip of his fingers.

"Help me!" he bellowed at the top of his voice as he bounced over the choppy wave tops. The flimsy wooden flagpole swayed and bent from side to side. It looked as if it might break at any moment.

"Man overboard!" shouted Al efficiently. Soon, her shouts brought people rushing out on deck.

"Hold on!" commanded Dither, taking charge. He leaped onto the guard rails. Then the tricky process of hauling the mighty mogul back on deck began. It proved to be no easy task...

At last the spluttering Scrupulous was safely hauled aboard. He collapsed on the deck, outraged. "Just what kind of boat is this?" he roared. "I come aboard expecting a nice relaxing break and what happens? – murder and mayhem, that's what!"

Then, swaddled in warm, dry blankets and clutching a large medicinal glass of Mythikan bouzo, Jolyon Scrupulous calmed down enough to tell his story. "I was out for an early morning stroll, mulling over an idea for a new kind of slug collar," he said, with a big barking cough. "I was leaning over the back of the boat watching the water."

"The next thing I knew – bam! – I felt a great big shove in the back. I lost my balance and over I went!" he concluded indignantly.

It's only by a stroke of luck I'm still here to tell the tale!

But someone on deck had no need to listen to Jolyon's story. Someone knew what had happened. Someone knew what the mega-millionaire was going to say before he spoke. But who? Who was the villainous perpetrator of the fiendish attempt on Jolyon's life?

Speedy Exits

Drops of rain began to spatter the deck as Jolyon finished his tale. By now, the boat was heaving in and out of the increasing swell. Dither hurried everyone into lounge B. He spoke solemnly. "We are in a desperate predicament!" To gasps of shock and horror, Dither spelled out the damage to the radio and engine.

 "Murder unlimited!" Dither continued gravely. "That is what we are dealing with. We must assume there have been at least three attempts – and some very narrow escapes." Swaying with the motion of the boat, he turned to face Jolyon Scrupulous. "Indeed, it is pure chance our friend is here at all!"

"Oh yes," continued Dither. "There is a villain in our midst. And he or she may strike again. But at who? If only we could find some connection between all these events. Alas, there is none!"

 "At the heart of the matter lies motive," pronounced Dither, staggering as the boat rolled first one way then the other. "And there is our problem," he said solemnly. "Find a motive, find a victim, find an opportunity – and, my friends, you find a murderer!"

Dither seemed to be losing his audience. The Captain was the first to bolt – but not the last. In ones and twos they tottered away...

...until only Al, Dan and Dither were left.

Dither turned to Al and Dan. "Now then, you two," he said bossily, with a twirl of his moustache. "I suggest you – "

Al and Dan waited patiently for him to continue. "Hrrrmph," he said, after a pause. Then, faintly, "Must go and er, splurrrg." And with that, he ran out of the room...

Judging by the green faces of their departing companions, Al and Dan were safe enough from any more villainy for the moment. Heads whirling, they tried to make sense of things.

"So, the first victim was Rula," said Al. "Then there was Mona. Last of all, Jolyon Scrupulous was pushed overboard. But why? What reason would anyone have?"

Dan was silent. Something Dither had said earlier was nagging away at the back of his mind. Something about Mona and the poison. Or was it about Rula and the snake? If only he could remember. He was sure it held a vital clue to the would-be murderer's identity.

"And what about the engine?" continued Al. "Who would know how to sabotage that? Then there's the mystery of the Captain's injury and the smashed radio. Dither says no one left any of the cabins!"

"What a puzzle," said Dan. "The only connection appears to be that there is no connection. But there must be one!" He paused, despairing. "The more we think, the more confused it gets. Let's start again. First, Rula was nearly murdered in her cabin."

"What did you say?" said Al.

Dan sighed. "I said, first Rula was nearly murdered in her – "

"But it wasn't her cabin," said Al. "Not to start with! Then Mona. Whose food did she eat? And the third attempt..."

"...was the right person!" finished Dan triumphantly.

Inside Cabin 5

Al and Dan staggered down to the cabin deck. It was hard to keep upright as the old boat battled through the heavy seas. They went straight in to cabin 5. This was no time to knock and wait.

It took a moment to attract the attention of the grumpy magnate. He turned around, frowning. Falteringly, Al and Dan explained their conclusions. His frown grew bigger and bigger.

"Preposterous!" said Jolyon Scrupulous. "I have enemies, of course. What person of power doesn't? And there are secrets here that could be worth a fortune to my rivals." The tycoon proudly waved a hand at a pile of neatly stacked boxes. "But murder? Who would dare?"

Suddenly, the boat lurched down into the trough of a particularly large wave. The pile of boxes started to wobble...

Once all the boxes were back in place, Jolyon Scrupulous knotted a length of strong cord tightly around them. Al and Dan tried once again to make him understand his life might be in danger. But it was useless. The mega-millionaire refused to listen.

"Nonsense," he snorted. "I, Jolyon Scrupulous, have the world at my fingertips. In any city in the world, all it takes is a phone call – and in ten minutes I can do anything! And now you tell me that some second-rate assassin is after me. Me! I think not!"

At that moment, there was a scuffling noise from the corridor. Was someone outside the door, listening to their conversation?

"A threat from the murderer!" gasped Al. She turned to Jolyon Scrupulous. His face had gone very pale. He seemed in a severe state of shock. For once, he appeared to have nothing to say.

Dan was puzzled. Somehow, it just didn't seem to fit. Would the ruthless villain who had carried out the vicious string of crimes really have written that petulant note?

Mona broke the silence. "One thing is certain, whoever tried to push you overboard must be watching your every movement," she began. "After all, it's very rare for you to get up so early. But who can it be? It must be one of your many enemies who is behind all these attempts on your life!"

"Ridiculous!" said Jolyon Scrupulous. "The idea of someone aboard trying to kill me! And do you think I would not recognize one of my enemies?"

Heading for Trouble

Clutching a bottle of Wundaworka, Al and Dan lurched out of cabin 5. They knocked on the door opposite. The boat was rolling and pitching heavily from side to side. How much worse could things get?

Rula greeted Al and Dan in a quavering and feeble voice. She gave up her struggle to read. Gratefully, she swallowed a dose of Wundaworka. Almost immediately, a tinge of pink returned to her cheeks.

"That's better," she said. "I'm trying hard to study for the second year of my soothsaying course. It starts in only two weeks."

The next stop was Cliff's cabin. He was just finishing a letter when they went in. He looked ill – and agitated.

Soon the Wundaworka took its effect on him. "If only everything was so easily cured," he said with a trace of bitterness. It was almost as if he was talking to himself.

Al and Dan left Cliff mumbling in his cabin. He seemed eager for them to go. On unsteady feet, they headed for Dida's cabin and rapped on the door.

Had she heard them knock? Swaying, Al and Dan waited – and waited. It seemed to be a long time before she answered.

At last Dida eased the door open a fraction. She looked flustered. Her hair was dishevelled. She didn't let them in, but stood clutching onto the door while she took the medicine.

"There's a storm ahead," said Al.

"You may be right," muttered Dida. "I fear you may be right."

There was no one in either of the other cabins. Clinging onto the handrails, Al and Dan went up the stairs. By now the wind was howling around the boat. Huge thunderclouds blocked out the sun. It was nearly midday, but so dark it could have been the middle of the night.

Al and Dan knocked at the door to the Captain's cabin. Max opened it. "They're both in pretty bad shape," he warned, letting them in.

Dan moved over to the two sickly chums. He got out the Wundaworka, then blinked. It was dark, but had a shadowy figure, or even two, just passed the window?

Dither recovered quickly. "Now, where was I," he said. "Who could the villain be?" He straightened his bow tie. "They say it's the quiet ones you should watch," he mused. "And, of course, often it's the least likely person – "

But the Captain had been listening to none of this. He had been studying the towering waves through the window. Now he spoke.

Suddenly, Al and Dan remembered the mysterious stranger on the shores of Loukaniki bay. What was it he had said about the tide?

Back in their cabin, Al made some quick calculations. She looked at Dan. "This will be the fifth turn of the tide," she said uneasily.

Dong! The ship's clock struck twelve. A huge streak of lightning lit up the sky, then a giant clap of thunder shook the boat...

The Storm

Would the storm never end? The Prancing Prawn floundered helplessly in the angry seas. Hour after hour, the gallant old boat was tossed and thrown around by the giant waves. The wind roared, the waves raged, and icy spray smacked down on the drenched and salty deck. All the passengers could do was cower in their cabins.

At last the storm began to ease. Al and Dan staggered out on deck. Then things happened thick and fast...

The door would hardly open in the wind.

There had been a few casualties.

Suddenly...

Look!

Al and Dan watched the Potted Shrimp drift away.

The dinghy!

Then the clouds burst open.

Al and Dan ran for shelter.

Did they hear a faint cry, whipped away by the wind?

Had that been the sound of running feet?

Inside, Al's foot touched something soft and squishy. . .

Under the Blankets

Al and Dan gaped down. A sodden bundle of old blankets at their feet started to move – and speak...

Then two dripping figures emerged, whimpering, from the pile of damp blankets. "Who-who are you?" gasped Dan. Before the pitiful pair could answer, the Captain and Dither arrived. Between them, they had plenty of questions for the trembling twosome.

The soggy stowaways seemed unable to say a word.

"Clap 'em in irons!" roared the Captain.

"Calm yourself, Russ, old boy," commanded Dither. "Now then," he said, to the dripping duo. "Let's start again. Who are you and what are you doing on this ship?"

"W-we are the Bungla brothers," said the one with the hat. "I'm Bala, this is Klava. We got a phone call yesterday from someone aboard this boat. We were hired to murder Jolyon Scrupulous!"

"But no one mentioned hurricanes," added the other Bungla bitterly.

"And might this be your calling card?" asked Dither sternly. He pulled a soggy piece of cardboard out of Bala Bungla's pocket and held it out for everyone to read.

Everyone read the words in silence. Then Dither spoke. "So, who hired you? When? And why?"

Once again, it was Bala who answered. "It all started at nine o'clock yesterday morning. We were sitting in Queezy-Sleezies, enjoying a malingo sling each and playing chek-choki..."

"The mystery caller gave us some instructions. When the crate arrived we took it to the boat, strapped it down, and left," continued Bala. "Afterwards, we sneaked back on board by climbing up the anchor chain. We hid in the crate. There was a lot of equipment inside – "

"The snake gave us a bit of a surprise," added Klava.

Once the Bungla brothers had started, they seemed only too eager to reveal everything they knew...

"And what about the anonymous letter?" asked Dither when the Bunglas came to the end of their list of dastardly actions. "And the other attempt on Jolyon Scrupulous?"

"What?" exclaimed Bala and Klava together. "We never – "

Just then Max burst in. "Something terrible has happened!" he gasped.

28

Some Interesting Reading

Max struggled to speak. "It's Dida," he sobbed. "She's nowhere to be found. She must have fallen overboard!"

Dither was quick to react. "Fallen... or pushed? Russ, gather everyone into the lounge. I'm going to search the boat for clues!"

While Dither poked and prodded his way around the cabins, Al and Dan told him everything they had discovered since they came aboard. "Hmmm. Interesting," said Dither, with a smile and a twirl of his moustache. "But I think you can leave the detective work to me."

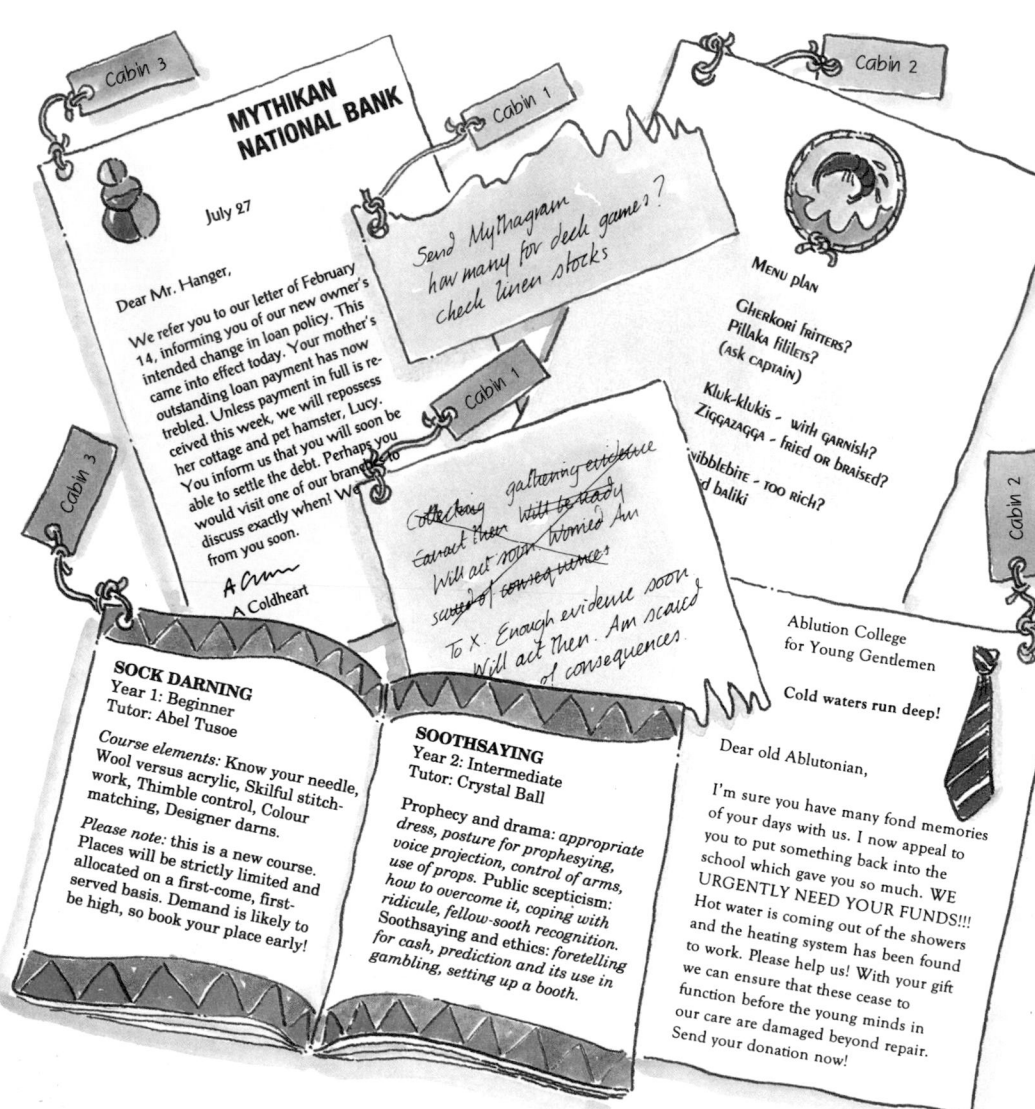

At last, every room had been searched. Al and Dan laid all the exhibits out on the dining room table. "Right," said Dither importantly. "Somewhere in here I'll find a clue to the mystery villain – the unsuccessful assassin who succeeds only in killing the wrong person!"

Dan thought about what Dither had just said. He was getting a glimmer of an idea. Maybe things were not quite what they seemed. And the bits of paper in front of them made some very interesting reading indeed. Had they been on the wrong track all along?

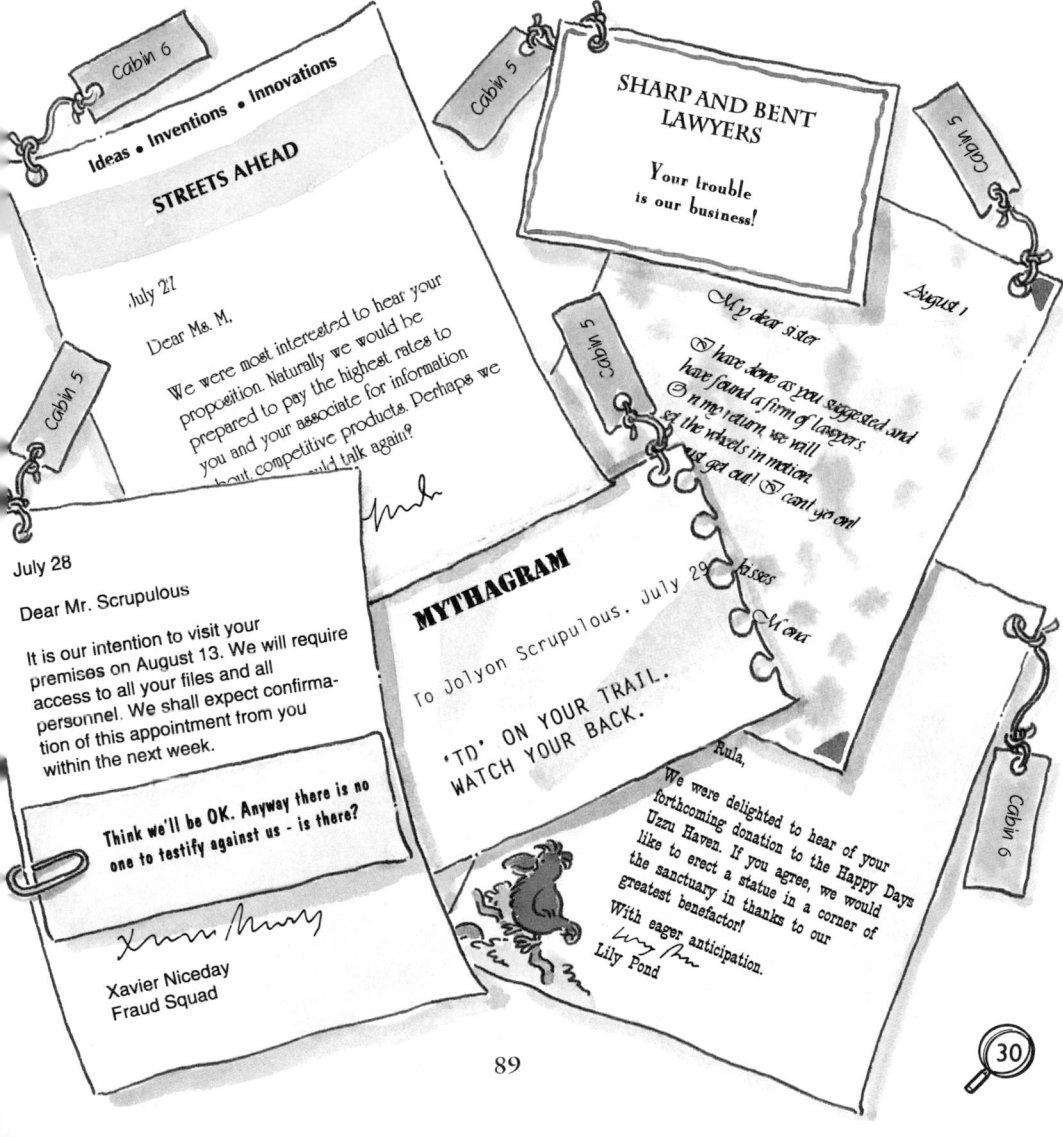

Cabin 6

Ideas • Inventions • Innovations

STREETS AHEAD

July 27

Dear Ms. M,

We were most interested to hear your proposition. Naturally we would be prepared to pay the highest rates to you and your associate for information about competitive products. Perhaps we ... ould talk again?

Cabin 5

SHARP AND BENT LAWYERS

Your trouble is our business!

Cabin 5

Cabin 5

My dear sister

I have done as you suggested and have found a firm of lawyers. In my return we will set the wheels in motion ... us get out! I can't go on!

August 1

... kisses
... Miora

July 28

Dear Mr. Scrupulous

It is our intention to visit your premises on August 13. We will require access to all your files and all personnel. We shall expect confirmation of this appointment from you within the next week.

Think we'll be OK. Anyway there is no one to testify against us - is there?

Xavier Niceday
Fraud Squad

MYTHAGRAM

To Jolyon Scrupulous. July 29

'TD' ON YOUR TRAIL. WATCH YOUR BACK.

Rula,

We were delighted to hear of your forthcoming donation to the Happy Days Uzzu Haven. If you agree, we would like to erect a statue in a corner of the sanctuary in thanks to our greatest benefactor! With eager anticipation.

Lily Pond

Cabin 6

Accusations Fly

Dither muttered and sucked in his cheeks as he read. At last he looked up. "Right. Some people have a lot of explaining to do," he said, heading for the lounge.

Al and Dan followed him. Things had become much clearer to both of them. It seemed that, all along, they had been busy thinking exactly the way the villain wanted – but no longer...

Dither stomped up to the shocked group huddled around the table. "A strange and brutal drama has unfolded before us," he began. "First, we have the Bungla brothers. A nasty pair of hired thugs, but small fry – the minor players. What we are after is the lead! Who is the fiend who hired the duo and then brutally took matters into his or her own hands? This villain must be found!"

"To that end we searched the cabins," Dither continued. "It proved most revealing. Coupled with what my young friends here have discovered, we seem to have some very guilty people in this room indeed."

"You see, my friends, we know everything," Dither continued. "What do you have to say for yourselves?" For a moment the wretched villains sat stunned, then they spoke anxiously in their defence.

He wouldn't remember Blubberface Kaloris. But I remembered him. Years at school he made my life a misery. When he chartered the boat I planned to get even.

We met at evening class. We discovered our common enemy and started planning. First Cliff got himself the job with Scrupulous. We saw our chance when the nanny's job came up.

We pretended not to know each other. That way no one would link us once the prototypes were sold.

You're wrong. That letter, those phone calls, they were about Sven Gayley, my producer. I'm trying to break my contract. I love my husband!

"It was wrong – but I only wanted to frighten him," said Max.
"My uzzus need a sanctuary. But murder – never!" said Rula.
"I only wanted to steal for mummy's sake," said Cliff.

The suspects all spoke at once. Dither was confused. "You all have reason to wish Jolyon Scrupulous harm," he said plaintively. "But reason enough to plot murder?" He rubbed his head. "Let me collect my thoughts. First, there was the snake, then the poison. Both were cases of bad planning, almost bound to lead to failure. This was the work of a second-rate villain – "

Al interrupted. "You're wrong. Someone is being very clever indeed – "

Dither glared at her and continued. "Next, the sabotage of the engine and the injury to our poor captain. Then the villain takes over from the Bunglas. And the sad result is, at the second attempt, a murder. Someone died – but the wrong someone! Although how anyone could mistake Dida for Jolyon Scrupulous, even in a torrential storm, is beyond me!"

"So there you have it," Dither concluded. "Someone in this room is lying, but who? Which one of you is the ruthless killer?"

Dan took a deep breath, then spoke. "All the pieces are in place," he said. "We know who did it, and why!"

STOP. DON'T TURN THE PAGE YET. You now have all the information you need to solve the string of contemptible crimes. Can you reveal the identity of the dastardly villain?

All is Revealed

Astonished, everyone stared at Al and Dan. Then Dither spoke. "How can you possibly know the identity of the killer?" he said. "We've had exactly the same information!"

"I'd like to hear what they have to say," interrupted Jolyon Scrupulous with a toothy smile. "It might be interesting."

To begin with, nothing made sense.

Nervously, Al began. "At first everything seemed unconnected – but there *had* to be a link somewhere. The first task was to find it. After the attempt on Jolyon Scrupulous it seemed clear that he was the target. It was only by pure chance the first two attempts had failed."

"Then we started to have doubts," continued Dan. "There seemed to be no one aboard with a true motive for murder. And there was something odd about the murder attempts. Had they really been serious? It seemed almost as if the villain wanted to fail. But what possible reason could he or she have? It was Dither himself who gave us the clue..."

... the unsuccessful assassin who succeeds only in killing the wrong person!

"But was it the wrong person?" said Al. "Look at the facts alone. Dida was pushed overboard. Just suppose that wasn't a mistake. If we stop assuming the target was Jolyon Scrupulous and assume instead that it was Dida, the attempt becomes successful!"

"Maybe all the time we were thinking along the wrong lines," said Dan. "And suppose that was because, for some reason, the murderer had made us do that!"

"Once again," continued Al, "It was thinking back to something Dither had said earlier that helped us slot things into place..."

... until we know what we are dealing with – and why – no one can be excluded.

"At the time, Dither meant that Mona and Rula could not be excluded from suspicion because they were victims," said Dan. "Yet later we all left one person off the suspect list, purely because he appeared to be the intended victim!"

"Don't you see?" said Al. "The attempts on Jolyon Scrupulous were a sham. They were meant to disguise the real murder – of Dida!"

"And only one person on this boat would have the deviousness to hatch such a fiendish plot!" said Dan.

"But why? We were stumped for a motive," said Dan. He tried to ignore the muttered comments around him, and continued. "Then we remembered the magazine article. Was it possible his former business partner, the holder of murky secrets about his shady dealings, had suddenly reappeared to tell all? If so, this could mean ruin!"

Al pointed accusingly at Jolyon Scrupulous. "You recognized Dida as your old partner and leaped into action! You set yourself up as the apparent target. Who would suspect you then? With your connections it wasn't difficult to do. A few phone calls secured the crate, the snake, the poison, the Bunglas. And just to make quite sure Dida didn't contact anyone, some sabotage – "

"Very clever," snarled the villain. "But where's your proof?"

"The Bunglas said the person who hired them had a strange voice," said Dan. "Among your prototypes is a voice transformer. You have the engine manual in your cabin. And I'm sure if we searched carefully, we'd find some trace of the sleeping drug you used on Mona when you went to meet the Bunglas and to carry out your monstrous murder!"

"Just now you said it was too bad no one on deck had heard Dida cry out," added Al. "How did you know anyone else was out on deck or that she cried out – unless you were there!"

"Clever – but not clever enough," said Jolyon Scrupulous with a sneer. "In case anyone was smart enough to figure it out, I brought this." He brandished a canister and ran to the door. "And outside my turbo-charged floatamota is waiting. Ha, ha!" the villainous magnate yelled. He pressed a button on the canister. The room began to fill with foul-smelling smoke...

Suddenly, a familiar voice came from just outside the doorway. "Not so fast, buster. Where do you think you're going?"

A Familiar Face

The clouds of trianide gas cleared slowly away. And there, framed in the doorway, stood Dida! She lifted her hand up to her head...

You thought you'd finished me off – but not so!

Then Dida began her tale. "The storm was easing when Jolyon Scrupulous burst into my cabin," she said. "He cried out that JJ was missing and rushed out on deck. I ran after him. Next thing I knew he was dragging me to the rails. I struggled hard but it was no use!"

"I was going down for the third time when something nudged me to the surface," Dida continued. "It was a friendly poropista – and a few feet away the Potted Shrimp was drifting by! I hauled myself aboard. Hours later, I was picked up by a fishing boat."

"I blurted out my story. Immediately, the fisherman chased after the Prancing Prawn. At last we caught up and clambered aboard. The fisherman went below to try and stop the engine. I followed the sound of voices. I got here just in time, it seems." She turned to Al and Dan. "But how did you guess who I was?"

"We noticed your tattoo when you came to your cabin door," said Dan. "We saw a strand of red hair as well, so we knew you were wearing a wig. And the magazine had shown a picture of Jolyon Scrupulous's partner with a tattoo and red hair! Then, later, Max mentioned your impression of the Captain. You used to be Teeny Dimple!" Dida blushed and nodded, then Dan continued. "The Mythagram in Jolyon's cabin clinched it. You had to be his missing partner!"

"Yes," said Dida. "We invented SLIME. It was a runaway success but that wasn't enough for Jolyon. He moved into dodgy business deals. After the Tuffaware take-over I threatened to report him to the fraud squad."

"Jolyon was mad with rage," continued Dida. "It seemed safer to disappear for a while. With the help of the fraud squad, I faked my death. I left my clothes on a lonely beach... But I still needed one last piece of evidence so I got myself this job – "

"I admit it," said a shamefaced Scrupulous. "I saw your tattoo as you picked up your hat when we first arrived. I panicked. Forgive me!"

Dida looked sternly at him, then spoke.

You have a choice. Give your fortune away – or go to prison!

94

Jolyon Scrupulous looked at Dida in amazement. Everyone waited in silence, wondering how things would turn out...

Detective Guide

This page will give you some help in solving the case. The numbers written here refer to the numbers inside the magnifying glasses found throughout the book.

1 Read the letter carefully. You might want to look at it again later.
2 Don't disregard the advice of the mysterious stranger.
3 Some of this information might be very useful.
4 Keep your eyes peeled here.
5 Take a good look at the smiling duo. You may not have seen the last of them.
6 An interesting book title . . . you wouldn't miss that again, would you?
7 If the Captain didn't order the crate, who did? (You won't be able to answer this now.)
8 Rula's luggage could be worth studying closely.
9 This odd discussion may make more sense later.
10 Keep your ears open here.
11 Who could that voice be hissing about?
12 Take your time over this.
13 Keep a close eye on things, particularly the preparations for the banquet.
14 Study all the statements carefully. Not everyone may be telling the truth.
15 Al has lots of questions. Can you answer any of them?
16 Al and Dan can't see as clearly as you can. Keep your eyes peeled.
17 Don't disbelieve Dither – he used to be a night-watchman.
18 Dither is right. What a lot of lucky escapes the potential victims have had.
19 Right again. At the heart of the matter lies motive – and you need a strong one for murder.
20 Can you remember what Dither said when he asked for everyone's statements?
21 Those prototypes are worth a fortune – to all sorts of people. And check out those boxes carefully.
22 Is this an idle boast? Maybe not.
23 Look at the note. Do you recognize anything?
24 At least one thing Mona says is right.
25 There's more to this page than might first appear.
26 A shadowy duo at the window – but who?
27 Could Dither be on to something?
28 The Bunglas could be giving away more information than they realize. Listen hard to their story.
29 Is Dither right? Or is he looking at things the wrong way round?
30 Read everything thoroughly. You might find some interesting new information – and don't forget about the importance of a strong motive.
31 Listen to the conversation of the shocked group at the table. Does this give you any more clues?
32 Would anyone really mistake Dida for Jolyon?

By the Way . . .

Now you've read the story and solved the mystery, check whether you spotted every clue. If you have difficulty reading this try holding the page in front of a mirror.

Did you spot the Prancing Prawn flying a red and white flag while at anchor on pages 52 and 53, instead of the normal Mythikan flag? This is an old Mythikan naval tradition, and is noted in the tourist brochure on page 55.

The Bunglas both had spotted neckerchiefs on page 57 but Klava's fell off when they went foraging for provisions (you can see it on the deck on page 59). They stole the melons from the galley and started scoffing as they went back. Klava noticed his neckerchief on the deck and picked it up, but in his rush to hide he left the end sticking out of the crate on page 62.

Did you see the copy of the Beginner's Soothsaying course book in Cliff's cabin on page 59? On page 82 Cliff and Rula both had a copy. So that was what they studied at evening class.

Did you recognize Rula from the photo in the Happy Days Hideaway brochure in her luggage on page 60?

On page 61 Mona had a mobile phone – a clue that she was not shouting at Jolyon, but down the phone.

On page 65 she came out of the changing room, again with a phone. This time she was talking to her sister, Nora. (There is a letter to Nora on page 89).

Did you get all the clues in the magazine pictures? The hand of Jolyon's former partner was resting on the car door frame, with a tattoo showing. Max was in the school photo wearing a Mythikan badge. And did you spot the sibilant's tail poking out of the tree?

On page 68. The clock next to it showed when they did so. Did you notice Mona say, "I eat like a bird"? Even Jolyon wasn't wicked enough to murder his wife. So he swapped plate with the only person he was sure wouldn't eat enough for the poison to work.

Did you recognize the silhouette of Bala Bungla in the engine room? If you were very sharp-eyed you might also have recognized his watch, first seen on page 57.

Jl was reading a book upside-down on page 80. The title should have given you a clue to the villain.

THE
MISSING
CLUE

Emma Fischel

Illustrated by Adrienne Kern

Series Editor: Gaby Waters
Assistant Editor: Michelle Bates

Contents

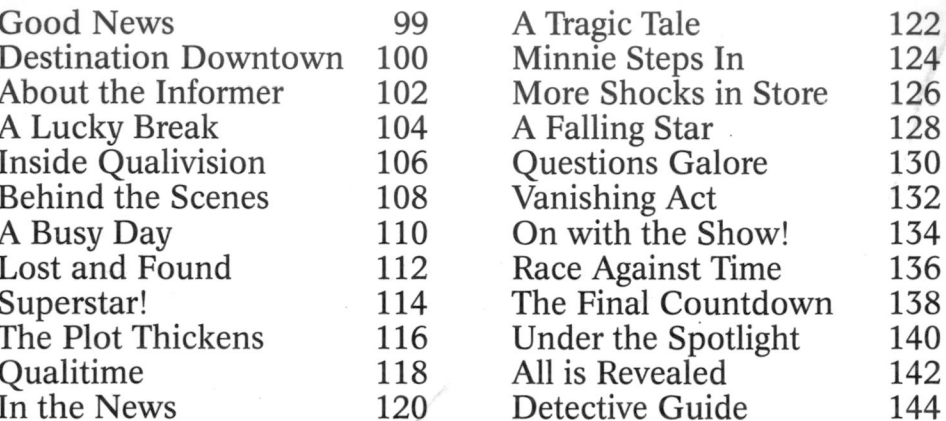

This is an exciting detective story that you can solve yourself. Clues and evidence are lurking on almost every page, but stay alert for red herrings that might put you off the trail. Vital information may be hidden anywhere, so make sure you read the text carefully. Look closely at the pictures and study all the documents and messages.

At various points in the book you will find this symbol ✎. When you see it, you can refer to the Detective Guide on page 144 for extra help. The guide will point you in the right direction and give you handy hints to help work out the mystery. By the end of page 139, you will have all the information you need to solve the case before all is finally revealed.

Good News

Hands trembling, Jack opened the package that had just arrived. He gasped. It was almost too good to be true. The first competition he had ever entered – and he had won!

His head spun as he read the details of the prize. For as long as he could remember, he had wanted to be a reporter. Now here was his big chance. And, who could tell, there might be a major story out there, just waiting to break . . .

Monday, October 5

CONGRATULATIONS, JACK!

You are the lucky winner of the CELEBRITY CHOMPERS competition!

We showed you six close-ups of celebrity mouths munching on TV Snax and asked you to name the stars. The only clue we gave you was that they were all up for Bravo awards this year. We also asked you to complete a tie-breaking slogan.

You, Jack, not only identified all the stars correctly but, in the opinion of our judges, yours was the best tie-breaking slogan!

Congratulations again, Jack! Now read on – and enjoy the prizes!

THE PRIZES!

Just look at what you have won, Jack!

A week as trainee reporter on Los Tamillion Informer, starting from Tuesday, October 20. Learn the ropes under the kindly guidance of Ed Lines, famous editor of Los Tamillion's number one TV mag. And – an added bonus – it will be during the week of the Bravos awards ceremony.

BUT THAT'S NOT ALL! You have also won

a year's supply of TV Snax!
a year's free TV viewing!

AND THERE'S MORE! We are enclosing

A TV Snax badge printed with your prize-winning slogan!
A free copy of last week's issue of the Informer!
A replica of the Bravos award so coveted by TV's greatest stars, perfect in every detail!

The CELEBRITY CHOMPERS competition was a joint promotion from the makers of TV Snax, the Los Tamillion Informer and the Bravos Committee.

TV Snax	The number one TV nibble lurking in everybody's kitchen!
The Informer	The ground-breaking weekly TV news and views mag. Wednesday isn't complete without it!
The Bravos	TV's most important award ceremony, attended by TV's most glittering stars!

The esteemed panel of judges scrutinize the thousands of competition entries that flood in. From left to right: Kris P. Nibble of TV Snax, Ed Lines of the Informer, Billy Banter, famous host of the Bravos.

WHEN HUNGER ATTACKS, REACH FOR TV SNAX!

THE BRAVOS
WHO WOULD YOU VOTE FOR?

Destination Downtown

Downtown Central station on a gloomy autumn morning . . . The rain bounced off the grimy streets like stray bullets off a tin can. A hungry cat scavenged for food among the bins. A car prowled slowly by, while, huddled in a doorway, Jack saw a solitary figure turn up his collar against the cold.

Outside the station, Jack hesitated. Could this really be the right place? Then, buttoning his jacket tightly and clutching his map, he set off down Ambition Avenue to find the offices of the Informer. A man scurried past him, umbrella pulled down low over his face to keep out the driving rain.

The street curved sharply to the right. Around the bend a grubby nameplate announced number 1013. This was it, and the door was already open. Inside, an iron staircase spiralled upward to a dusty skylight way above. Jack's feet echoed loudly on the worn stone steps as he made his way to the third floor.

The Informer office seemed a busy place. No one heard Jack knock and no one noticed as he pushed open the door and stood, dripping, in the doorway. After a moment he coughed politely, then coughed again, this time a little louder.

At last a woman swathed in lilac turned her head. "Yes?" she said, tucking a pencil neatly behind one ear.

"I-I-I'm the competition winner," Jack said nervously. "When hunger attacks, reach for TV Snax . . . I'm here for a week as my prize."

"Is that so?" said the lilac vision, scrutinizing Jack from head to foot. "You'd better see the boss, then. The door over there," she said, jerking a finger in the direction of the far end of the room. "Knock, then wait. Oh," she added. "And good luck . . ."

About the Informer

E d Lines, ace newshound, glared out at Jack from behind a cluttered desk. "So you want to be a reporter," barked the famous journalist. "Well, let me tell you, you're starting at the top with the Informer!"

With that, the magazine mogul eased himself out of his swivel chair and strode over to a vast portrait hanging prominently on the wall. "Mother," he announced proudly. "She created the Informer. She dreamed of building the greatest magazine ever about television and its stars – the best articles, best photos, best everything. And she did it! From the very first issue, she got all the major scoops and stories. No other paper could compete."

"And it all started from here almost thirty years ago," continued the media tycoon, slapping his hand down hard on his battered old desk. "We've never moved since. Everything is still just the way mother had it."

"But fifteen years ago mother was called to the great gossip column in the sky," said Ed. He paused to blow his nose vigorously, then continued. "I took over. For years I have dreamed of handing the Informer down the generations, but it seems destined not to be."

Dabbing at his eyes, Ed Lines rummaged about in a drawer. "Here. Read this," he said, handing Jack a bulky document.

THE INFORMER

The Informer, founded 27 years ago, quickly established itself as the number one magazine for television news and gossip. A weekly magazine that comes out every Wednesday, it is still widely read today. It was the brainchild of Isabel Lines, widow of Alfie Lines, the famous ventriloquist. Isabel founded the magazine at the age of 50, encouraged by her children, Edmund (then 20) and Christabel (then 15). The first issue was an instant sell-out, breaking the story of the split of two of the most famous TV stars of the day.

Isabel Lines died at the age of 62. Her son, Edmund, took over as editor of the Informer and continues today, 15 years later. The Informer still operates from the same offices of its humble beginnings in the Downtown Central district. In an interview just before her death, Isabel Lines confessed to her dream of the Informer carrying on as a family-run business, but sadly, it seems the Lines dynasty is not destined to continue.

Very first issue

Family trouble

Isabel Lines with her children 20 years ago

Fifteen years ago Edmund's sister, Christabel, cut all contact with her brother. This followed a fight over her refusal to join the Informer on the death of their mother. After 11 years of silence Christabel wrote to Edmund from far-off Mythika, telling him he was now uncle to a three-year-old girl and suggesting a reunion. Tragically, that was the last Edmund heard from her. He has since had no success in tracing her.

Edmund's daughter, Arabella (from his marriage to actress Posy Bouquet), chose to follow her mother into the acting profession. She shows no interest in taking up the leadership of the Informer. Because of this, she and her father no longer speak to each other.

Biggest scoop

Ten years ago the Informer broke all circulation records with photos of top star Drusilla Dazzle in a dramatic drenching incident. It stemmed from Ms. Dazzle's involvement with the ill-fated musical tragedy, Dreamaway. On the opening night her co-star was taken ill and the understudy, Bob Swing, took over. But he ruined the play by forgetting his lines and altering the course of the plot, throwing the rest of the cast into complete confusion.

The critics savaged the play and it closed after one night. Drusilla used her influence to ensure Swing would never work in Los Tamillion again. Some months later, he burst into the restaurant where Drusilla was dining. He stormed up to her table and emptied the contents of a flower vase over her head, then left town, vowing revenge. An Informer photographer on the spot got exclusive pictures of the whole incident and the public flocked to buy copies. It became the Informer's biggest selling issue.

Biggest seller ever

A Lucky Break

R-r-ring! The shrill noise of the phone cut through the silence in the room. "Yup," said Ed tersely into the receiver. "What! No . . . how long? Disaster!" With that he hung up, scowling.

"So you want to be a reporter?" he said again. "Well, here's your chance. May Kittup, our star reporter, has just broken her toe. She won't be in for a while and no one else is free to take over her story. It's about Workout. We want a story on the show to tie in with the Bravos."

To: May Kittup
From: Ed Lines
Date: October 13
Ten days to the Bravos. We need a story for our bumper Bravos issue. Suggest you get down to Qualivision and do a feature on Workout and the Bravos. Interview the stars that are up for awards, find out about Workout's past wins and losses, see what preparations they are making for the ceremony. Get me any information you can.
Have attached a few recent bits of info which may help. Report in to me with progress each morning.
Good luck!

Qualivision — the TV channel that brings you hits such as Workout, Timeshare and Teen Trivia from its Los Tamillion Studios.

Sam Smarm, publicity department.

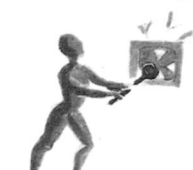
TV in a class of its own!

Qualivision TV studios
1-111 Media Mile
Los Tamillion West

* SHOW NEWS * SHOW NEWS * SHOW NEWS * SHOW NEWS *
WORKOUT - TWO YEARS ON TOP!

TV's highest rated soap is coming to the end of its second great year. And the number one from Qualivision is also up for five Bravos to add to the three it has already. That's more nominations than any other show!

It is almost two years since viewers first tuned in to the comings and goings of everyday life in a busy sports and leisure complex. The show has since become an institution, capturing the imagination of the public and touching the hearts of millions. Will Coach leave for pastures new? Will Dan ever forgive Daisy? All these and more are questions the public wants answered. And they will be, so keep tuning in!

Rock Solid plays Coach
Luke Martin plays Dan

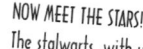

NOW MEET THE STARS!

The stalwarts, with us from the beginning and – we hope – to the end, need no introduction *Rock Solid,* known to millions of viewers simply as "Coach".
Luke Martin, idol to young people everywhere as athlete Dan Drummond.

Drusilla Dazzle plays Billie
Bella Bouquet plays Anna

Hello to our newest recruits, bringing fresh life to the show in October:
Drusilla Dazzle plays ferocious new owner of the Workout complex, Billie O'Nair.
Bella Bouquet plays her fresh and lovely young assistant, Anna Peel.

And last but not least, that famous feline friend of the viewers, *Pawprint.* A true star – and he behaves like one! He will eat only Meaty Morsels (Chunky variety) and lies only on a patterned silk rug, which must always be tucked in the same way before he will sleep on it.

BRAVO MANIA!

It's that time of year again, when the nation tunes in to see who will win – and lose – TV's most coveted awards. On Friday, October 23 at 7pm, two hours of awards and entertainment will be broadcast live to millions of homes around the globe. Yes, it's Bravo time once again!

Fraser Storey, last year's winner for Best Play, Backstabbers. Said Fraser: "For 10 years I've dreamed of winning a Bravo – but I never expected it would be for writing!"

A win can transform a career. Last year, Fraser Storey (pictured above) found his dreams came true after his win for TV drama. Previously a complete unknown, the next day he was offered a plum script-writing job for Workout, TV's highest rated soap.

"First thing to do is show the Workout team the photos we took at Friday's rehearsals. They have to approve them before we use them," Ed continued. "Then find out all you can about Workout and the Bravos." He handed Jack an envelope. "This should help start you off."

Jack opened the envelope. There were the four photos, plus a couple of newspaper articles. Workout . . . the Bravos . . . what a combination – TV's number one soap and the biggest awards ceremony known to the world of television!

HIJACKED

September 30

Soap war bubbles over! Shock double move by Dru and Bella!

Dru and Bella go out to celebrate newly signed contracts with Qualivision.

Goodbye Terminal! We're off to Workout.

Drusilla Dazzle and Bella Bouquet today announced their departure from Terminal, the popular twice weekly soap about life in a busy airport. They move next week to Workout, which recently nudged Terminal into the number two position in the TV soap war. Both stars deny any truth in reports of constant battles on the soap set over who has the greater number of lines, more close-ups and better scenes. Said Drusilla last night, "Bella and I are good friends. Don't believe everything you read!"

TUG-OF-LOVE
MINNIE TIPPED FOR TOP

Minnie Marvel is tipped for an award at this week's Bravos for her portrayal of tug-of-love Viola in Workout. The nomination has a tragic poignancy, as in real life little Minnie is an orphan. Four years ago, Minnie and her mother were kidnap victims. One of the kidnap gang, struck by remorse, helped them escape but, tragically, her mother fell over a cliff.

Plucky little Minnie doesn't remember much about it. "We were kept in a dark, smelly room. A nice man helped us escape. When mother fell over he carried me to safety along a tree branch wedged on the waterfall. I was scared. It was very high and the branch was very narrow, but he didn't seem to mind at all."

Minnie's father never recovered from the loss of his wife and soon passed away. His step-sister, Cosima Charade, took Minnie in. "Minnie begged me to let her go on the stage," says her devoted guardian. "And after all she had been through, how could I refuse?" How fitting that little Minnie is now in line for a major TV award. What a worthy winner!

2

Inside Qualivision

The train screeched to a halt. Through the window Jack could see the station sign: Media Mile. This was the stop for Qualivision. The train doors opened with a hiss and Jack got off.

Outside, the skyline was dominated by a huge building that stretched way down the street. Hundreds of windows glinted in the feeble rays of the winter sun. Jack clutched the envelope Ed had given him tightly to his chest and headed for a revolving door set high up a wide stone staircase. He pushed the door open and stepped inside the headquarters of Qualivision, the most famous TV studio in Los Tamillion . . .

Jack's shoes squeaked loudly with every step he took across the vast expanse of marble flooring. He arrived at the reception desk in the corner. "Excuse me," he stuttered, nervously. "I'm looking for the Workout studio."

"Guided tours every Tuesday, two o'clock," droned the receptionist.

"N-no," stumbled Jack. "I'm here on business . . . from the Informer. I'm expected. I –"

"You'll need to see Thea Trickell, then," interrupted the receptionist. "She's in charge."

"How do I find her?" asked Jack.

"Try turning around," said the receptionist, pointing her expertly manicured finger in the direction of the sofa.

. . . and Minnie simply refuses to do the pool scene. She throws a tantrum every time we mention it.

. . . about Drusilla and Bella. Make sure our two new stars have plenty of exciting scenes!

. . . Luke's acting was dreadful yesterday. Could you write in an accident – give him some time in the hospital. That'll soon improve things!

Mmm, that is a problem.

Uh-huh. I'll see what I can come up with.

Just a moment. Dratted pen – always leaking!

4

Jack took advantage of a pause to introduce himself. Thea Trickell leaped up. "Splendid!" she said. "Come and show everyone the photos." Heels clicking busily on the floor, she swept out of the hall, talking hard. "Let me tell you a bit about us," she said. "I am producer and director of Workout."

This is it. The Workout studio!

"Which means she runs the whole show," interrupted the man with the leaking pen, panting in her wake. "Anything she says goes."

"That's Fraser Storey," said Thea beaming. "He writes each episode." Then she stopped outside a door.

Behind the Scenes

Thea Trickell took a deep breath. "Attention!" she roared. Awestruck, Jack watched the stars immediately form an obedient group around their leader. "Three days to go to the Bravos," began Thea. "And I have some exciting news. The organizers have asked us to perform a short scene during the ceremony. It will be seen around the globe in thousands of countries. This means worldwide publicity for Workout."

"Over the next few days press interest will be high," continued Thea. Then she turned to Jack with a smile . . .

Already, we are graced by the presence of the newest recruit to the Informer. Jack, meet the Workout stars.

. . . Rock Solid, who plays Coach, one of our most popular characters.

. . . Bella Bouquet, who has just joined us as Anna Peel.

. . . Minnie Marvel, our delightful little child star, who plays Viola.

. . . Luke Martin, who sets hearts fluttering as talented athlete, Dan Drummond.

"And, of course, there's Drusilla Dazzle," added Thea. "But she's out representing Workout at a theme park opening today."

"Jack is researching an article on Workout to tie in with the Bravos," Thea continued. "Please give him all the help you can. First, he has some photos for you all to look at." Jack handed them around.

Tee hee. Look at Minnie!

Hmmm. Got my bad side.

Drusilla doesn't look too happy.

I'm only in backview.

"Enough!" said Thea briskly. "To work. We need to rehearse the new scene for the Bravos. Remember, only three more days to go."

A Busy Day

Fraser Storey handed each of the actors a copy of the short scene he had written for the Bravos ceremony. He started to speak. "Right, here's what happens. We start with Minnie alone on stage. She's playing with a boxing glove. All of a sudden, Coach bursts in. He's agitated beyond belief . . ."

Fraser waved his pen back and forth as he outlined the scene. Red ink leaked from the nib and dribbled down his arm but he seemed not to notice. "Then – wham! – the curtain comes down," he finished triumphantly.

"Marvellous!" exclaimed Thea. "Let's read the scene through. I'll take Drusilla's lines." And so the first rehearsal began.

From a seat in the corner of the studio, Jack watched the rehearsal speed by. Then he queued with the actors for lunch in the Qualivision canteen.

Precisely forty-five minutes later everyone was back in the studio. Rehearsals continued for an hour, then a rail of glamorous clothes was wheeled in through the door. "Time to choose an outfit for the Bravos," said Thea to the cast. "You can take your pick from any of these clothes, courtesy of Qualivision."

Decisions proved hard to make but at last everyone was satisfied they had found the perfect outfit for the great occasion. "Five o'clock," announced Thea. "That's it for now. Time to go home."

Ten minutes later, Rock was the first to go. Bella and Luke left soon after him, followed swiftly by Minnie and her guardian. Then Thea looked at her watch and gasped, "Five-twenty. I must dash!"

Jack picked up the envelope Ed Lines had given him. It felt light – very light. Puzzled, he pushed his hand inside the flap. Where were the photos?

What can I do? he thought, quaking. And what on earth will Ed Lines say when he hears I've lost the photos?

Lost and Found

At last Ed Lines ran out of insults. "This is not a good start to your second day," he snarled. Grabbing a grubby folder from his desk, he started to leaf through the pages inside. "OK Office Supplies ... Pablo's Pasta ... It's in here somewhere," he muttered. "Ah-hah! 'Paparazzi Printers. Open nine to five, seven days a week.' That's the one."

"They printed the photos," Ed explained. "They still have the negatives, so we can get copies." With that, he picked up the phone and dialled. Minutes later he slammed the phone down. "We're too late," he said, perplexed. "Someone went there yesterday – said they were from Qualivision and needed the negatives of the Workout session. The printers never thought to question them."

"Whoever it was must have seen the printers' name stamped on the back of the photos," Ed mused.

Then Ed stopped, interrupted by a sudden cough from the doorway...

Ed Lines got out two large cigars. "So what brings you over this way, Will?" he asked the craggy-faced private eye.

"Big trouble, Ed," sighed Will Pry. "I need your help, and fast. Remember this?" He slapped a piece of paper down on the desk...

the names
tv stars
offspring?
our survey
can reveal
this year
popular
for girls:

Whimsie
Sparkle
Porcelain
Chiffon
Pizazz
Moonshine
Starlette
Cosmos
Vitality
Beluga
Eternity
Shimmer
Blushes
Chemise
Alopecia
Pomegranate

WHERE ARE THEY NOW?

This week we ask for your help in tracking down a bunch of ruthless criminals known as the Spotlight Gang. Over the last few years, a wave of seamy showbiz crimes has shocked the citizens of Los Tamillion. Remember the Mogul Mansion burglary, the Dynamite Duo kidnapping, the Replica Ruby blackmail case? The Spotlight Gang is believed to be responsible for them all!

The gang's roots can be traced back at least four years. Their first known victims were child star Minnie Marvel (while still an unknown) and her mother, kidnapped in a tragic case of mistaken identity. The gang snatched the unlucky pair outside a museum in Mythika, believing them to be glamorous star Iva Bigg-Brake and her daughter, Ava. Upon discovering their mistake, they decided to dispose of the two in the Intrepid River, but were foiled by a member of the gang who has since disappeared.

Since that early bungled attempt, the Spotlight Gang has become increasingly dangerous. They need to be stopped! Our sources now believe that they are closer to rounding up the gang than ever before. But they need your help to make the streets of Los Tamillion safe for us all. Does this picture jog any memories? If you have any information, please contact us. Our office is waiting for your call!

continued from page 7.

also a child, who would now be seven. The only real clue we have lies in a letter, written from Mythika four years ago. It was the last letter ever received from her. Below we print an extract from it. Anyone with any information should contact the Missing Persons Hotline.

-3-

...can't imagine. I rushed out of the house to see her, drenched, with the empty bucket wedged on her head and her left arm stuck in the guttering. She said she had been trying to find out about the crime. Still, the scar (a strange kind of crescent shape) should fade with time. And I'm sure she'll get over her fears - at the moment she's so scared of water she even drinks through a straw! Anyway Ed, that's all my news. If you are prepared to let bygones be bygones and go along with my plans for a reunion, please contact me in Mythika. You and Archie will have so much in common and your little niece is longing to meet you.

All love, Christabel

"You ran this three weeks ago. Thanks to that we have new evidence," said Will Pry, pulling some photos out of his pocket. "We want to put these in every paper we can. They are from Elsa Storey, the eminent Mythikan plastic surgeon. By chance she saw that issue of the Informer, left by her brother over from Los Tamillion. She recognized the faces at once. It seems she did some work on the gang leader four years ago – these photos are after surgery. Elsa Storey says all but one of the gang had surgery of some kind. She was the perfect choice for their plans. She had just been abroad on a specialist course for three months, and hadn't heard about the kidnap. So she performed the surgery, not knowing she was helping wanted criminals. The gang then left Mythika and moved their crime base to Los Tamillion, complete with their new appearances, and free from fear of discovery."

"She has photos of them all before and after surgery, except one who changed his mind about treatment. She can't find his photo, although she knows she had one. A pity – but the leader is the one we really want."

Ed took the photos then turned to Jack. "Still here?" he barked. "Get down to Workout. And don't make any more mistakes!"

Superstar!

Outside the Qualivision building, Jack was startled by a sudden loud toot on a car horn. He jumped aside as a long black car with smoked glass windows screeched to a halt at the foot of the steps.

Drusilla Dazzle! Jack followed, awestruck, as the superstar swanned gracefully up the steps and into the Qualivision building.

"Flowers for you, Miss Dazzle," twittered the receptionist.

The glamorous star of stage and screen threw a sweeping glance around the hall. She caught sight of Jack hovering by the door and waved an imperious arm at him. "You there, bring them to my dressing room," she commanded.

Staggering under the weight of the enormous bouquet, Jack stood on the threshold of the star's dressing room. Drusilla Dazzle beckoned him in. "I daresay you want my autograph," she said, graciously. "Everyone does."

Picking up a leather-bound volume on her dressing table, the superstar smiled kindly at Jack. "I keep a store of photos tucked in here for my fans," she said. The book was full of old photos and press clippings. "My life has been a fairy tale," she sighed, lost in thought as she turned the pages. "Oh yes, I've had it all. Fame, fortune . . ."

Times were hard at first. Night after night in the chorus line. Then one evening fate took a hand – the star and understudy got food poisoning. I was pushed on stage to take over. That night was to change my life.

I became a star! Life was a glamorous whirl of parties, premières – and suitors. But I only had eyes for one man. Then came a hideous magazine article. Not one word was true, but the stubborn fool refused to listen. That was the last time we spoke. Nearly thirty years of silence . . .

Still my career scaled yet more glittering heights. I won award after award. My Etta in Showtime was hailed as a masterpiece, the best ever. Then came disaster, my first and last musical, Dreamaway. It closed after one night. But happier times were to follow – and another Bravo. How I wept!

The superstar dabbed at a tiny tear glistening in the corner of one eye. Just then, there was a rap on the door and a voice called out. "Drusilla, you're needed at the Bravos press interviews."

The Plot Thickens

Studio 3 was packed. Drusilla took her place on the podium while Jack squeezed into a seat at the back of the room. Then Thea started the press session. But events were soon to take a dramatic turn . . .

Bewildered, Jack watched as the Workout team, led by Luke, helped themselves to copies of the paper that had just landed in a thick bundle on the floor. What was Qualitime?

Thea saw his puzzled face and picked up an extra copy. "Take a look," she said, handing it to him. "Everyone at Qualivision reads it."

QUALITIME

QUALIVISION, TV'S BEST AND BRIGHTEST CHANNEL

Today, a special word from Ivan Inkling, your managing director.

Greetings, everyone! This Friday sees a very special day – the thirtieth anniversary of the Bravos. Yes, the greatest of TV awards ceremony is upon us once again.

And each year, one of the most consistent presences, with winners galore, has been Qualivision! Let's hope this year turns out to be no exception.

To celebrate this thirtieth year of the Bravos, we look back at some past triumphs from Qualivision – and forward, we hope, to some future ones.

So, welcome to a special Bravos edition of Qualitime!

30 YEARS OF QUALIVISION AND THE BRAVOS

30 years of laughter and tears, winners and losers. We look back over some of our most successful Bravo years.

*Year 1. Best comedy award: Rock Solid and Drusilla Dazzle in Qualivision's **Hush my mouth!***

*Year 20. Best actress: Drusilla Dazzle in Qualivision's **Grit**.*

*Year 29. Best TV drama: Qualivision's **Backstabbers** (shown here in rehearsal).*

In the first year of the Bravos, Qualivision scooped best comedy award. Rock went on to star as Jed Slim, cowboy hero of the popular TV series, Gun Shy (repeated 20 years later and just as popular!). Drusilla had only recently shot to stardom, and was soon destined to become a household name, known to millions as Leila in Travesty, the long-running saga of the Midas family.

Drusilla wins again for Qualivision 20 years later for her no-holds-barred portrayal of wronged widow Faith Anhope. Qualivision's Grit, a tale of one woman's rise to fame, fortune and power against all the odds, came only months after she starred in the ill-fated Dreamaway. Dreamaway may have ruined the career of her co-star, Bob Swing, but Dru certainly managed to rise above it!

Best TV drama was one of a clutch of awards Qualivision gained last year. Just over a year ago Qualivision spotted Fraser Storey's potential and was brave enough to take a chance on an unknown. The reward was a searing drama of the backstage, backbiting world of the acting profession. Gossip raged as to who the characters were based on but our number one writer is not saying anything..!

I n the canteen, nearly everyone was reading Qualitime. Jack browsed through his copy while he munched a sticky bun, on the lookout for information that might prove handy for his article . . .

Wednesday, October 21

QUALIVISION, TV WITH GUTS

Today, a little reminder to you all. Successful though Qualivision is, we still have to watch those pennies! In the interest of Quali-conomy all phone calls are now logged, and have been for the past week. From now on, each department will get a daily list of all calls made. The list will show the time and length of the call, and the number called (including those made to other Qualivision departments). I shall examine these lists daily. So keep those calls short, and let's have no more time wasted chatting to friends in other departments or auntie in Ohio. You have been warned!

Time for our daily word from Jenny, Qualivision's general manager.

THIS YEAR'S HOPES

Qualivision has nominations in almost every category this year:

  Best TV drama: No Way Out
  Best comedy: Timeshare
  Best daytime drama: Workout
  Best children's presenter: Susie Slapstick
  Best documentary: Beginners Please!
  Best actor: Rock Solid
  Best newcomer: Bella Bouquet
  Best supporting actress: Minnie Marvel

And a special mention for Drusilla Dazzle who this year collects a Lifelong Devotion award, for her contribution to quality programming in the arts. Well deserved, Dru!

Best children's presenter, Susie Slapstick, wacky host of Splat!

Best documentary: the first week for new pupils at Precocia Stage School.

⒀

The rest of the day passed in a whirl. Jack asked question after question about Workout and its stars. By the end of the day his notepad was packed with scribbled information. At last, exhausted, he went home to bed.

In the News

The Informer office was practically deserted when Jack arrived the next morning. He switched on the battered old television in the corner and the morning's news stories began to filter quietly into the room. Settling himself at an empty desk, Jack opened his reporter's notepad and looked through his last two day's notes.

Workout
Goes out twice a week (Tuesdays and Thursdays at 7:30pm) on Qualivision.
Has been running for two years.
Actors get their scripts for each week on Tuesday morning. They rehearse and record from Tuesday to Sunday, 8am-5pm.
They have Mondays off.
(This week they came in on Monday as well because of preparing for the Bravos.)
They work on episodes two weeks ahead of the ones we see on TV.

Qualivision
TV channel which has been going for 33 years. All shows made by Qualivision studios.

Rock Solid
First appeared as a carrot in a commercial for Soupy Sauce Mix.
Made his name as Jed Slim in Gun Shy. Also films and stage work but career faded for a while when he got a reputation as unreliable after split with Drusilla Dazzle.
Did a lot of charity work for Broken Hearts Anonymous. Made a comeback when old episodes of Gun Shy reran 10 years ago. Suddenly became cult figure and in demand again. Landed part of Coach in Workout two years ago. Has been in show since first episode.

Luke Martin
First big break was as Ryan Keen in Kid Cop nearly 4 years ago.

Has played Dan Drummond in Workout since episode 10.
Before that, lot of travel to different countries - his parents were a circus trapeze and high wire act.
Luke joined the act 6 years ago but left suddenly after 2 years and moved to Los Tamillion.
Only Workout star not in line for Bravo award.

Drusilla Dazzle
Has been almost constantly in work ever since pulled out of chorus line and made a star. Only flop in her career was Dreamaway.
Has taught regular acting classes at Would-Beez Academy for Young Actors for nearly 10 years.
Says she knows she has been fortunate and hopes she can pass some of that good fortune by helping young actors learn their craft properly.
Is frightened of small dogs.

Bella Bouquet
Grew up in Los Tamillion. Always wanted to be an actress but strong opposition from her father.
Took various jobs to put herself through drama college. Has not spoken to father for two years.
First stage job two years ago. First TV was Terminal. Moved to Workout at same time as Drusilla Dazzle, two weeks ago.
Likes hot air ballooning.
Does voluntary work for Missing Persons Hotline.

Things to find out
Ask Fraser how he gets ideas for plot. When did he start writing? What made him start? What did he do before?
See if Thea will tell me more about stars. Things like who is easy to work with, who is difficult; who gets along with whom; are there many arguments between actors? And anything else she can think of.

14

Jack sighed. Being a reporter was not as easy as it seemed. He had plenty of information, but where was the story to go with it? If only something really interesting would happen –

Suddenly Jack looked up at the television. Something the newscaster was saying had caught his attention . . .

A Tragic Tale

There was no time to waste. Jack was out of the door and heading for the station in seconds. This is it, he thought, as he bounded aboard an uptown train. My first scoop! But he was not the only one on the trail of the story...

A crowd thronged the Qualivision steps. How would Jack ever get through? Just then he heard a familiar voice behind him. It was Will Pry! The private eye propelled Jack to the front of the crowd.

Seconds later, the guard waved them inside. "I found his lost parakeet," explained Will tersely. He sprinted along the maze of corridors that led to studio 3. Then he pushed open the door.

The comic panels at the top contain the following speech:

Panel 1: "And go away – no, it's no use. The line's all wrong."

Panel 2: "OK, Bella, here's another idea. How about . . ."

Panel 3: "Take the cup, drink, then say . . ."

Panel 4: "Never darken my door again!"

Panel 5: "And then you slam the cup down . . ."

Panel 6: "Ooops."

"Then Pawprint lapped up the spilled liquid," finished Thea. "And, two minutes later, he died." She blew her nose loudly. "They've just carried him into the ambulance. Now all that's left is an empty basket."

Fraser patted her arm, then moved over to the abandoned basket. "It's too sad a reminder. It's upsetting you, I'll move it," he said kindly.

(15)

"Stop right there!" ordered Will Pry. "Where are the actors? I need statements from everyone."

"Nothing moves without my say-so!"

Thea sniffed. "They all went to their dressing rooms. At least, I know Bella and Drusilla did. They're very shocked."

Will turned to Jack. "You stay here. Remember – no one touches anything!" Then the three of them left.

Jack heard a scrabbling noise in the roof. Rats, he thought, shivering. It was eerie to be alone in the studio . . . But was he?

(16)

Minnie Steps In

Pssst!

Jack spun around to see Minnie Marvel beckoning mysteriously. "Follow me," she said. "I may have a clue about the poisoner." With that, she headed off for a corner of the studio.

Perplexed, Jack followed her. "I want to be a crime reporter," explained Minnie, "so I'm gathering evidence for my first big story. I haven't got the answer yet. But there seem to be plenty of suspects," she added darkly.

What was she talking about? thought Jack, confused. Then, dimly, he heard more rustling from the roof. Those rats again . . .

"I hate being an actress," sighed the chattering child star. Suddenly she slithered underneath a rail of clothes tucked away in a dark corner.

"Cosima put me on the stage," Minnie's voice continued, muffled, from under the rail. "She's my guardian, my father's step-sister. There's no one else to look after me. Well, I think my mother had a brother but they didn't speak." Then she emerged, flushed with success and clutching a small suitcase.

 There was a loud bang as the studio door shut. But surely it had been shut already – could it have blown open?

Inside this box there's lots of important information.

After a moment Minnie continued. "This is my evidence box," she announced, brandishing the battered old suitcase with pride. Then she clicked open the lid.

Amazed, Jack peered inside at an array of things belonging to the Workout team. For a moment he hesitated, then he started to read. It's a reporter's duty not to overlook information that comes his way, he told himself firmly. It's how you use it that matters.

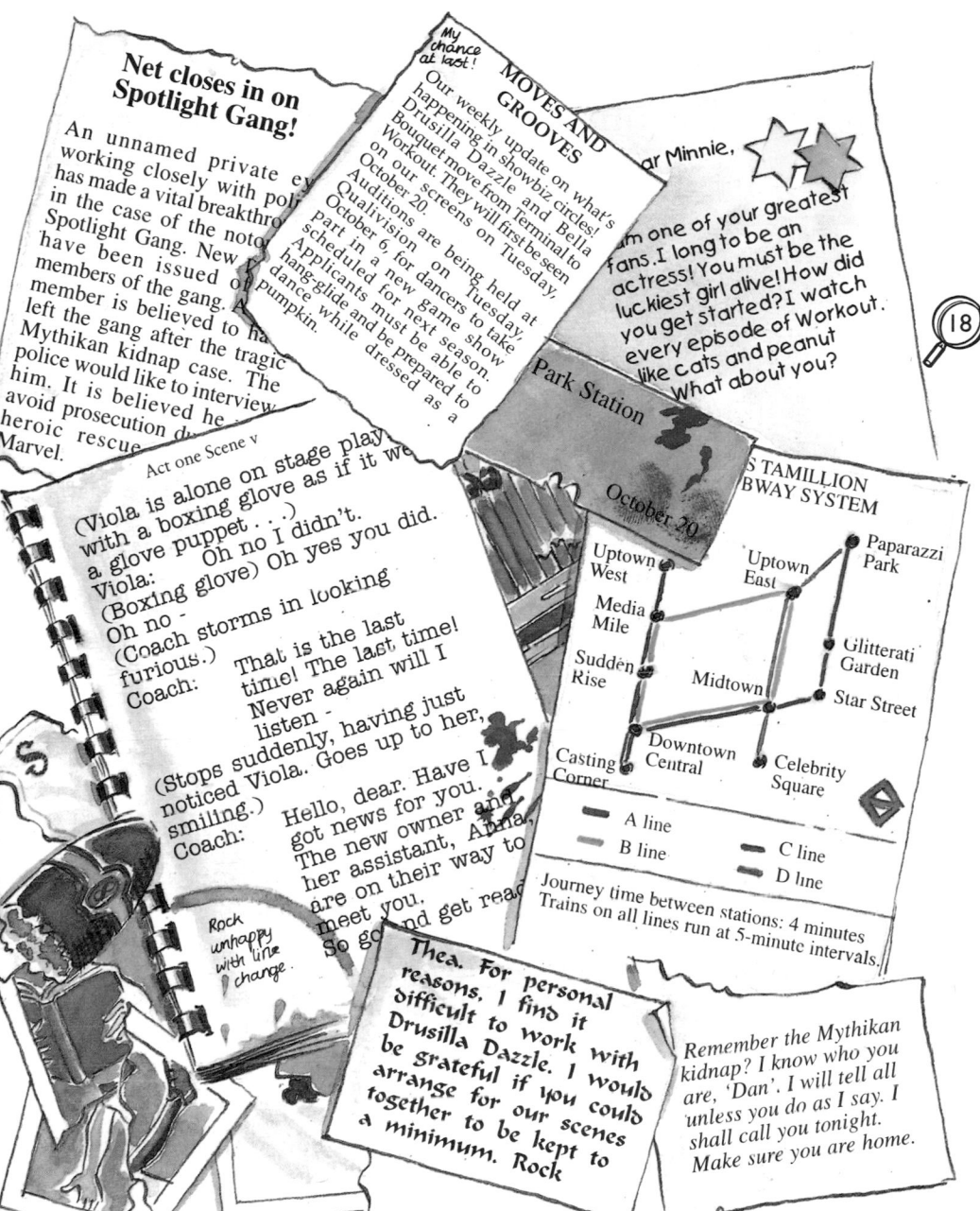

Net closes in on Spotlight Gang!

An unnamed private e... working closely with pol... has made a vital breakthro... in the case of the noto... Spotlight Gang. New... have been issued o... members of the gang. A... member is believed to ha... left the gang after the tragic Mythikan kidnap case. The police would like to interview him. It is believed he... avoid prosecution d... heroic rescue... Marvel.

My chance at last!

MOVES AND GROOVES

Our weekly update on what's happening in showbiz circles! Drusilla Dazzle and Bella Bouquet move from Terminal to Workout. They will first be seen on our screens on Tuesday, October 20.

Auditions are being held at Qualivision on Tuesday, October 6, for dancers to take part in a new game show scheduled for next season. Applicants must be able to hang-glide and be prepared to dance while dressed as a pumpkin.

...ar Minnie,

...m one of your greatest fans. I long to be an actress! You must be the luckiest girl alive! How did you get started? I watch every episode of Workout. ...like cats and peanut... What about you?

(18)

Park Station

October 20

S TAMILLION BWAY SYSTEM

Uptown West · Uptown East · Paparazzi Park
Media Mile
Sudden Rise · Midtown · Glitterati Garden · Star Street
Casting Corner · Downtown Central · Celebrity Square

— A line
— B line
— C line
— D line

Journey time between stations: 4 minutes
Trains on all lines run at 5-minute intervals.

Act one Scene v

(Viola is alone on stage play... with a boxing glove as if it we... a glove puppet . . .)
Viola: Oh no I didn't.
(Boxing glove) Oh yes you did.
Oh no -
(Coach storms in looking furious.)
Coach: That is the last time! The last time! Never again will I listen -
(Stops suddenly, having just noticed Viola. Goes up to her, smiling.)
Coach: Hello, dear. Have I got news for you. The new owner and... her assistant, Anna, are on their way to meet you. So go... d get read...

Rock unhappy with line change.

Thea. For personal reasons, I find it difficult to work with Drusilla Dazzle. I would be grateful if you could arrange for our scenes together to be kept to a minimum. Rock

Remember the Mythikan kidnap? I know who you are, 'Dan'. I will tell all unless you do as I say. I shall call you tonight. Make sure you are home.

Jack sifted his way through the contents of the suitcase. There was plenty to read and at the bottom of the pile, he found some scraps of glossy paper. There was something familiar about them. He pulled them out for a closer look . . . the missing photos, torn up! Just then, the studio door creaked open.

More Shocks in Store

Through the doorway came a giant bouquet, carried by a staggering delivery boy. Another followed, and then another. By two o'clock Pawprint's basket was surrounded by tributes from a devastated public who had by now heard the ghastly details of his death by poison.

Then the Workout team arrived. Shocked and distressed, they were all still unable to talk about anything but Pawprint's tragic demise.

Oh, it's too sad. Let's move it.

No. Leave it - a fitting tribute to an eternal professional.

"Never liked the critter but never wished him harm," sniffed Rock. "A poisoner among us? Surely not!" said Drusilla. "How could anyone be so cruel?" wept Bella. "If only he hadn't drunk it," sighed Luke.

For a moment there was silence. Everyone stared sadly at the shrine to the feline fatality, then Thea gathered herself together. "We must put this behind us," she said bracingly. "The show must go on. Think of the Bravos. It's what Pawprint would have wanted."

While preparations got under way for the rehearsal, Will Pry beckoned to Jack. "I found some interesting things just now, kid," said the private eye. "But I need more evidence. We're dealing with a major star here." The sleuth put a heavy hand on Jack's shoulder. "Problem is, I have another big case at the moment. I need you to . . ."

He was just about to say more when Thea called for silence. And so work began again on the ill-fated scene that had led to Pawprint's untimely death. For a few minutes things went smoothly, until . . .

Crrrk! A heavy arc light creaked ominously above the Workout team. Seconds later, it hurtled down from the ceiling. For one terrible moment it seemed certain to the horrified onlookers that Bella would be crushed beneath it. Then Fraser Storey, in a lightning-quick move, pushed her out of the way. The light whistled past her head and crashed to the ground. (20)

"I could have been killed," gasped Bella. She lay sprawled on the floor, deathly pale.

Will Pry spoke. "Something mighty strange is going on around here. This makes one narrow escape too many. It's time to act!"

A Falling Star

Will Pry knelt down and examined the light closely, muttering under his breath. Then he stood up and made a startling pronouncement. "This was no accident. This was a cold-blooded attempt at murder!" Amid gasps of disbelief from every corner of the studio, Will Pry continued. "The metal ropes have been part-sawn through. This is the latest in a whole series of attempts on the life of an innocent young girl."

"In the first attempt," the private eye continued, "the lights fused. A lucky chance, or deliberate sabotage – who can say? But, whichever it was, someone seized the opportunity."

"The villain grabbed Bella, intending to strangle her, but lost courage. Fearing time would run out, the culprit ripped off the necklace to make it look like robbery." By now Will had everyone's complete attention. "The next time, careful planning went into the attempt," he said. "It was only Bella's problem with her lines and Fraser's intervention that saved her from Pawprint's fate."

"The villain was becoming desperate," continued Will Pry to his rapt audience. "The arc light was risky – there was no absolute guarantee it would land on Bella – but it was worth a try."

The private eye scanned the room. "But who?" he asked. "And why? Everything pointed to an insider, to someone who knew the schedules, knew the way script rehearsals and recording worked."

And so I began my investigation.

"I turned up some interesting finds," continued the sleuth. "A book on poisons. Fragments of a broken bottle bearing traces of tedium hypochondriade, a deadly substance when drunk. And, most significant of all, some broken metal rope, used by the villain to work out how far the ropes would need to be sawn to make them snap at the right time. All these things were in one dressing room. But whose?"

"You had me fooled to begin with, lady," Will Pry said to Drusilla. "I let you blind me to the truth. But no more! It was a sad case of professional jealousy turning to terrible crime. One star threatened by the meteoric rise of another – it's a common enough story in this town." Before anyone could respond, there was a loud rap on the door and four police officers walked in. Will Pry nodded in the direction of the dumbfounded star. "There's the culprit!" he said.

Handcuffed and chalky-faced, Drusilla was led away. Everyone stood, stunned, as the door swung gently to a close behind her. Something stirred at the back of Jack's mind. It was as if he had just been reminded of something important as he watched Drusilla leave. But what was it that had made his mind race? Just then, Will Pry's phone started to ring.

The private eye talked fast, then the conversation was over. "Kid," he said, turning to Jack. "Get back to the Informer. Let Ed know what's happened. And tell him, if all goes well, I may soon have a scoop for him on the Spotlight Gang." Will Pry headed for the door. "I gotta go," he said. "The net is closing on a truly wicked bunch of criminals." With that, he pulled his hat low over his brow and left.

Questions Galore

What a scoop!

Ed was beside himself with excitement. "Tell me again," he urged. "From the fused lights to Drusilla's arrest. I want to hear it all!" Jack went through it once more.

"And Bella is unharmed, you say?" queried Ed anxiously. As Jack nodded he rubbed his hands with glee. "What a story! What a tie-in with the Bravos!"

Ed rushed happily back to his desk, but Jack was worried. It seemed to him that many of the things that had happened over the last few days just didn't add up. He wasn't convinced that Will Pry was right. But what could he do about it?

He sat down with a sigh. He felt something in his back pocket. The photos! Why not stick them back together, he mused, digging out all the scraps. After all, their disappearance was the first thing to happen in this strange saga.

Hmmm. How about – "Workout star in horror vendetta! Will Bella quit showbiz for ever?"

No, no. Let's try – The Informer says: Get out Bella, it's not safe in showbiz!

Jack stared at the photos he had pieced back together. There were only three. He had a scrap from the corner of the fourth photo. But where was the rest of it? Things were getting more and more puzzling.

Jack's head was teeming with questions. Why would anyone steal the photos? Then why tear them up? What had been in the one that was missing? Was there something important about it? Could it have a link with everything that had happened since?

The more he thought, the more confused he felt. He got out his notepad and tried to make sense of it all. An hour later, he looked at the jumble of unanswered questions on the page in front of him. Oh well, he sighed, packing up to go home. What more can happen now?

Is Drusilla really guilty? Why would she risk ruining her career? Is her motive convincing? She wouldn't have had time to fuse the lights and do the strangling, so did she rely on chance? Or did she have an accomplice? Is she the person most likely to have had access to a Mythikan poison? When could she have sawn through the light ropes? (Not while Minnie and I were in the studio - she was in her dressing room.) And what about Will Pry's evidence against her? Is it really conclusive?

1) Strangling. Haphazard.
Relied on chance light fusing. If it didn't, two people must have been involved - one to fuse lights, other to strangle.

2) Poison. Painstakingly planned.
Will Pry had it examined: some kind of Mythikan poison. Who would have access to it? Need to plan carefully to get hold of. Would have succeeded if Bella hadn't objected to her lines. Cup filled at 9am. Cat died at 9:10, so only ten possible minutes. All Workout team could have done it. Who had most opportunity? Would anyone have found it easy to do without being noticed?

3) Arc light. Risky.
No real guarantee of when light would fall and that it would definitely land on Bella.

Could the noise Minnie and I heard in the roof have been the villain at work on the light? If so, can we eliminate anyone as not being villain - was anyone definitely not up in roof at the time?

Seem to be three very different kinds of murder attempts. Not much in common. None of them would be guaranteed of success.
Could there be another link between them apart from Bella as victim? And why is Bella the victim anyway - who would have a grudge against her? Seem quite dramatic, showy sorts of crimes. Does that tell me anything about the kind of person that might have planned them?

What about the things in Minnie's bag? Would it help to look at them again?
Subway ticket: station name partly obscured by ink blot. Should I try and work out what station name is? Is the date important?
Moves and Grooves clipping. What does the message mean? Who wrote it?
Personal ad. Why does it seem so familiar?

THE PHOTOS - WHY, WHY, WHY would anyone steal them? And why is one still missing?

23

Vanishing Act

The big day had dawned at last. The evening would be filled with the excitement and glitter of the Bravos. But now it was cold and foggy. It was still early and most of the streets were silent and deserted. Only a few shops were beginning to open their shutters as Jack set off, bleary-eyed, for the Workout studio.

Speeding along in an uptown train, Jack fretted once more over the arrest of Drusilla Dazzle. But he soon had something else to think about. Outside the Qualivision building a huge crowd of reporters was gathered around the steps, hurling questions at the security guard: "Any news?" "Any comment?" "Any idea where he might be?"

Jack was bewildered. What were they all talking about? Just then a news vendor shouted out: "Workout star in no-show drama! Read all about it!" Jack fumbled for some change and grabbed a copy of the paper. Staring out from the front page was a very familiar face.

A close friend commented, "It seems most unlike Luke. He is always so reliable." He was seen leaving the Qualivision building yesterday afternoon, clutching a copy of Qualitime, and muttering, "No more! No more!" Friends are at a loss to explain this comment.

Luke in his first TV role, as Kid Cop.

The last reported sighting of Luke Martin was in Queen Street by little Frank Donaldson. The tiny tot was crying because his kite was stuck in a tree when the star passed by. Living up to his athletic TV image, Luke vaulted high up into the tree, then walked along a narrow branch as easily as if he was on the ground. He untangled the kite then shinned down the tree and ran off, obviously in a hurry.

Little Frankie Donaldson – the last person to have seen Luke Martin?

Daily Tittle Tattle

MISSING! TOP STAR IN REAL LIFE DRAMA

TV heart-throb Luke Martin in his current role as athlete Dan Drummond in Workout.

News came in late last night of the sudden mystery disappearance of Luke Martin, young star of top TV show, Workout. The teen idol was due to turn up yesterday evening at the Yahboos, the music industry's answer to TV's Bravos, to present the award for best new act to young band, Glug. He never arrived. Speculation is growing as to his whereabouts. For full story, see back page.

Luke missing! It was almost impossible to believe. Aghast, Jack hurried up the steps. The security guard recognized him and waved him through. Inside studio 3, everyone seemed to be in a state of shock.

It was all too much for the stricken cast and crew of Workout. They seemed unable to think of what to do next. But just then the door burst open and in marched Will Pry. He looked very grim-faced indeed as he started to speak.

The private eye took a sheet of paper out of the envelope he was brandishing. Everyone crowded around to read it.

It certainly made for some very interesting reading. You could have heard a pin drop while they took in what it said.

By the time you read this I will be thousands of miles away. Do not try to find me. Someone there will understand what I'm doing and why.

I confess to my part in the crimes against Bella. Drusilla is innocent of everything. I never dreamed things would go this far. I am despicable, but even I have a point at which I must stop. I will do no more. I have done enough already.

Luke Martin

On with the Show!

After the first shocked reactions, the voices died away. No one could believe what they had just read. It seemed too incredible. Then Thea broke the silence. "So, Drusilla is innocent. She must be released at once!"

"It's all in hand," said Will Pry. He seemed a little edgy. "The lady should be here any time now. I wasted no time in getting her release once the letter arrived." Tugging down his hat, he turned to the door. "Anyway, I gotta scram," he continued. "Thanks to my efforts, the notorious Spotlight Gang are cooling their heels in a cold cell. They're in need of some serious questioning." With that, he turned up his collar and left the studio fast.

Minnie tugged on Jack's sleeve. "Listen! I have some vital information," she said urgently. "It was when I saw Pawprint's rug, that was when I knew. And I was right!" But Jack was listening to raised voices in the corridor outside the studio. The door flew open.

"Drusilla!" gasped everyone, as she burst into the room, seemingly unbowed by the shattering experiences of the last twenty-four hours.

"I'm back!" announced the star. "And just in time to spot that fool of a detective slinking away down the corridor. Imbecile!" She paused dramatically. "And now to work!"

134

"But Luke played a big part in the scene. Can we get something else ready in time? We have nothing prepared," said Thea doubtfully.

Fraser had been writing feverishly ever since Will Pry had told them the news of Drusilla's release. Now it was his turn to speak. "Let's turn this disaster into triumph!" he declared, jumping up and waving a script around. "We'll give the Bravos a scene to remember. We'll make it really dramatic, give Drusilla the central role," continued the scriptwriter, his eyes aglint with excitement. Then he began to explain his idea to a spellbound audience.

You argue, then you aim the gun at Drusilla.

BANG! It goes off, the lights dim, the curtain comes down . . .

And no one knows if she lives or dies!

Never were lines learned so quickly! They rehearsed the scene again and again until, at last, Thea was satisfied. "Congratulations, cast," she beamed. "Tonight, the show will go on after all!"

Everyone cheered. Only Drusilla seemed deep in thought, speaking so quietly that only Jack could hear. "It's ten years," she murmured. "But I'm almost sure . . ."

And there's the ring as well.

Please listen to me!

What was she talking about? Jack was filled with a deep sense of foreboding. Then Minnie pressed something into his hand. The missing photo!

"Just look at the time," Thea exclaimed, looking up with a gasp. "Only four hours until the Bravos!" Jack followed her gaze up to the clock perched above the phone booth, then he glanced back down at the photo. All at once, he realized exactly why it had been so important for someone to conceal it. And the proof was right here in his hand.

135

Race Against Time

Time was running out. Ignoring Minnie's pleading behind him, Jack raced out of the studio. Next stop was the Qualitime office.

Up three flights of stairs and along a corridor that seemed to stretch for miles, at last he reached the offices of the Qualivision daily newspaper. Seated behind a large desk was a portly receptionist. His eyebrows shot up as Jack explained what he wanted.

... back issues from ten years ago ... and last week ... phone record ... personal ads ...

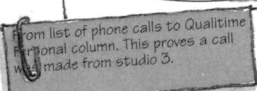
From list of phone calls to Qualitime Personal column. This proves a call was made from studio 3.

TOP OF THE FLOPS

We had no idea what we were starting when we invited you to nominate your worst show this year from stage, screen or TV. Your nominations came flooding in.

Today we can reveal that the runaway winner, with over one-third of all the votes cast, was

DREAMAWAY! A stage spectacular that fizzled out after just one night.

Drusilla Dazzle in the worst career move of her life. Will she recover from this disaster? One thing's for sure, her co-star won't - she's made sure of that!

Bob Swing, taking his first and last step into the limelight. What will he do now? Time for a career change, Bob!

By now, the whole story of the disastrous first and last night of the musical tragedy, Dreamaway, has gone down into theatrical folklore. Those of you who were there say it is a night you will never forget - largely due to the efforts of one man, Bob Swing. In his role as the Dream Maker, he managed to turn the evening into a nightmare for the cast. Even a seasoned old pro like Drusilla couldn't hold the show together. Unfortunately, what was meant to be a tragedy turned into a comedy, with most of the audience hysterical with laughter. But no one in the cast was chuckling when the reviews came out the next day and closed the show.

Friday, October 16

Outside number: 603860013
Time: 2:51
Length of call: 8 mins

Internal number: 254 (Studio 3)
Time: 3:00pm
Length of call: 6 mins

Outside number: 701731222
Time: 3:07pm
Length of call: 2 mins

Internal number: 171 (Accounts)
Time: 3:09pm
Length of call: 3 mins

Internal number: 409 (Personnel)
Time: 3:23pm
Length of call: 5 mins

Outside number: 808174983
Time: 3:34pm
Length of call: 13 mins

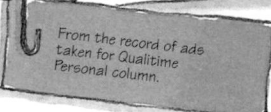
From the record of ads taken for Qualitime Personal column.

Day: Friday
Date: Oct 16
Method: Hand delivered
Time: 2:40
Message: Amelia. Come to a party at my house tonight. I shall cook you a meal to remember.

Day: Friday
Date: Oct 16
Method: Phoned
Time: 3:00
Message: Remember the Mythikan kidnap? I know who you are, 'Dan'. I will tell all unless you do as I say. I shall call you tonight. Make sure you are home.

Day: Friday
Date: Oct 16
Method: Hand delivered
Time: 3:10
Message: Visit Chuckles 'n' Chocs for novelty gift ideas for the star 'who has everything'.

It took a while to convince the bemused receptionist to help. But at last, an hour on, Jack was armed with all the information he needed. Then he raced downtown to the Informer office. Sitting at his desk, he hurriedly laid everything out in front of him.

> I only hope I'm not too late. This may be a matter of life and death!

Let's check I'm right first, he thought. There are things I still need to puzzle out. I must be sure before I act.

Remember the Mythikan kidnap? I know who you are, 'Dan'. I will tell all unless you do as I say. I shall call you tonight. Make sure you are home.

'Dan'. Instructions are where I told you. Follow them exactly. Don't fail me or I shall be forced to talk to the police.

'Dan'. This time more complicated. Two jobs for you. New instructions in the same place. Don't fail me or you know what will happen.

'Dan'. Hello again! Another little task for you. Make sure you carry it out. Instructions are in the same place.

From last Monday's issue. Could it be useful?

IN THE PIPELINE

From Sam Smarm, Publicity Department

Exciting news! Qualivision plans to make a miniseries of the Minnie Marvel kidnap. We have no word yet of who is up to play the major roles. Little Minnie is, of course, now too old to play herself as a three-year-old.

Hotly tipped for the role of Minnie's mother is Bella Bouquet. When Minnie was asked her opinion, she said "Bella would be good. She reminds me of my mother. They have the same sort of smile and they laugh the same way."

As far as actors to play the members of the notorious kidnap gang, only a stunt man has been chosen so far. He will be needed for the dramatic final rescue scene where little Minnie is carried to safety by one of her kidnappers. In an accurate reconstruction of the real rescue, the stunt man will have to carry Minnie (a dummy will be used) over a narrow tree lodged between two sides of a waterfall. One false move and the stunt man will hurtle thousands of feet down into the fast-flowing Intrepid River.

One wag in our department has suggested that Luke Martin would be ideally suited to the role. With his childhood background of circus skills we might even save on the stunt man fee!

(28)

By the time he had finished reading, his worst suspicions were confirmed. Minnie had given him the one vital piece of evidence that proved his story – the photo. But where on earth could she have found it?

Quaking at the thought of what he had to do, Jack jumped up. There was no time to worry about that now. If his guess was right, the villain had one last dastardly act planned, a fiendish crime that would take place this very evening in front of thousands and be beamed live to countless watching nations around the globe. Somehow, the Bravos must be stopped!

The Final Countdown

At that moment, Ed Lines walked in. "What's up, kid?" he asked, seeing Jack's worried face.

"There's going to be a murder at the Bravos," burbled Jack. "Unless we stop it. But how can we get there in time? And –"

"Whoa," said Ed. "Start again, and this time, make sense." Then he listened while Jack told his story. When Jack had finished, Ed looked at his watch. "We have forty-five minutes," he said. "To the Bravos – and fast!" And so began a frantic race against time . . .

STOP! DON'T TURN THE PAGE YET. You now have all the information you need to solve the string of dastardly doings. Can you reveal the identity of the fiendish felon?

Under the Spotlight

Drusilla screamed. Startled, Rock jerked the gun up to the ceiling. There was a deafening crack, then the auditorium was plunged into darkness.

Seconds later, the beam of a spotlight started to rove around the room. It swept up to the balcony and came to rest on Jack. All eyes turned to him. "Drusilla Dazzle," he began. "Someone loaded the gun intending that you should die tonight. That person was Fraser Storey!"

Gasps could be heard all around the auditorium. Jack pressed on. "Why should Fraser want to harm you? Because he is none other than Bob Swing, the actor who ten years ago starred with you in Dreamaway, and ruined the show with his incompetence. You made sure he never acted again, so he vowed revenge – and tonight he very nearly got it."

"But Bella . . ." began Drusilla.

"Fraser staged the attempts on Bella's life too," Jack cut in. "He didn't really want to kill her at all; he wanted to frame you as the would-be murderer and see you sent to prison. When his plans failed, he decided to turn to murder himself!"

Suddenly, a voice cut through the darkness. "An interesting theory, young man," said Fraser Storey. "But tell me, do you actually have any proof for your fanciful accusations?"

"I most certainly do," said Jack, pulling something from his pocket. "You gave yourself away when you chose an accomplice for your crimes."

The photo was the vital missing clue.

"You found out that Luke Martin had been in the Spotlight Gang and used blackmail threats to force him to help you. Those ads you put in Qualitime for him to see – I knew they had something to do with the attempts on Bella's life. I saw in the company log when the calls had been made to place the ads. But it wasn't until I saw the photo of Friday's rehearsal which showed you making a call that I had proof that you were the culprit. The photo matched the time and number in the company log. After that, everything fell into place."

"Not so fast," said the voice from the darkness. "You may have your proof – but I have a hostage!" The spotlight swung around to reveal the frightened face of Minnie Marvel. "Yes Drusilla, I did want my revenge," continued Fraser, enjoying his moment of power. "Just because I had stage fright and forgot my lines, you made sure my career was over. So I formed my plan – I would ruin you as you had ruined me."

"I didn't know why you seemed so familiar," said Drusilla in wonder. "Then your ring jogged my memory. You always used to wear it . . ."

"The strangling attempt was meant to frame you," interrupted Fraser. "Pawprint's poisoning, too. I knew Bella would object to that scene. How simple to drop poison in the glass and break it while demonstrating her new lines! The arc light was risky, but I was ready when it fell to make sure no one was harmed. And it was easy to plant the evidence when I went to your dressing room with Will Pry."

"Then there was Luke." Fraser was unable to stop now. "He got involved with the Spotlight Gang but left as soon as he could. He was the one who rescued Minnie. Shame he can't do it again, eh?" He smiled as he tightened his grip on the little girl. "Luke moved to Los Tamillion and thought he was safe. The only photo of the gang the police had was so blurred he thought no one would ever know. How sad for him that I visited my sister Elsa – the plastic surgeon who operated on the gang – and found she had a photo that showed him clearly. So I contacted him. What a waste of time he was . . ."

All is Revealed

Thump! Thud! Crash! The sounds of a tremendous scuffle echoed down from the lighting gallery. The lights flooded on and feet thundered down the stairs. Then Fraser Storey appeared, dragging Minnie Marvel, and with Luke Martin in hot pursuit. Luke flung himself forward and hurled Fraser to the ground. "Gotcha!" Luke gasped. "I knew I was right to come back!"

"You again!" shouted Fraser. "You've ruined everything –" He drummed his fists on the floor in frustration.

"If only I'd thrown away those photos," he sniffed. "I tore them up and threw them away, then I panicked. Suppose someone found the vital one? So I stuffed all the pieces of it – except one bit that I couldn't find in time – into Pawprint's basket. I planned to destroy them later."

"But someone else got to that vital photo before you did," Jack pointed out. "Minnie Marvel."

Minnie beamed proudly. "I knew something was in Pawprint's basket," she explained. "His rug was all messed up."

"Foiled by a child!" muttered Fraser through gritted teeth.

"Fraser Storey, I have heard everything," said Will Pry, emerging from the audience, with two police officers following. "I arrest you for . . ."

"Stop!" interrupted Drusilla. "I am not blameless in all this. I have long regretted ruining Fraser's acting career as I did. And now, thanks to his scripts, Rock and I are working together again after so many wasted years. That is worth more to me than anything else. Fraser, I shall not press charges!"

I have something to say!

Fraser looked up, astonished. Tears of gratitude began to stream down his face. Just then, a quiet voice said, "Errr, what about me?"

Seems to me you've paid your dues, son.

It was Luke. He looked nervous. Then Will Pry spoke. "Your heroic action today and your role in the Minnie Marvel kidnap rescue should excuse you from prosecution," he said. The gripped Bravos audience gave a loud cheer.

Meanwhile, Ed Lines turned to Bella Bouquet and held out his hands. "Daughter dear, I'm sorry for our silence of the last two years. I realize that acting is the right thing for you. Will you forgive me, Arabella? I know now that not everyone can want to be a reporter."

It's my life's ambition.

"But *I* do," chirped a small voice behind him. Minnie babbled on but Ed was staring at her arm. "How did you get that scar?" he asked.

"In an accident when I was three," said Minnie. "I got my arm stuck in some guttering." To everyone's astonishment Ed Lines burst into tears. "Then you must be my long-lost niece!" he sobbed.

Just then, Will Pry's phone rang. He listened intently then spoke, beaming. "A woman has been found up the Intrepid River. She says she fell over a cliff four years ago and was rescued by mountain yetis. She has lived with them ever

My auntie! My sister! My mother!

since and only just recovered her memory. Her name is Christabel Lines!"

We have witnessed a strange drama of our own on this stage. But now – let the Bravos continue!

Detective Guide

This page will give you some help in solving the case. The numbers written here refer to the numbers inside the magnifying glasses found throughout the book.

1 Take your time over this. It could prove useful later. Don't forget to look at the pictures closely.
2 This could be worth studying carefully.
3 Take a good look at this scene.
4 Keep your eyes open and listen carefully to Thea.
5 Listen hard here. Some of this may not mean much now, but try to remember it.
6 There are some interesting reactions to the sight of those photos.
7 There's more to this page than might first appear.
8 So everyone has chosen an outfit for the Bravos – or have they? Are you sure?
9 It could be a good idea to make a note of those opening times.
10 There may be some enlightening new information here. Read everything carefully.
11 The pictures may lend a hand here.
12 Look closely at this page, then think hard about what – and whom – you have seen.
13 Can you sort out the information to see which bits are useful?
14 Jack's notepad may be more helpful than he realizes.
15 A tragic tale indeed. Keep your eyes and ears peeled.
16 Rats – or could it be something else?
17 Those sort of doors don't blow open, do they? So what's the alternative?
18 This page could be very revealing. It might help if you work out who all the handwriting belongs to.
19 You too could take a good look at the shrine to the feline fatality. Has anything changed?
20 A very lucky escape indeed – or was it?
21 Will Pry may be closer to the real truth than he knows, but perhaps he is looking at things from the wrong angle.
22 It might help to take another look at the pile of information Ed Lines first gave to Jack.
23 It is worth trying to answer as many of these questions as you can.
24 Does anything in this article trigger off any memories of another dramatic incident in the past?
25 Keep your ears open here.
26 Listen hard to what Drusilla is saying.
27 By now your brain should be starting to tick . . .
28 Are things becoming clearer? If not, try looking back at pages 103 and 105 for more help.
29 A grudge – against whom?

By the Way

Now you've read the story and solved the mystery, check whether you spotted every clue. If you have difficulty reading this try holding the page in front of a mirror.

Did you notice that Pawprint's blanket was all scrunched up on page 126 – something the feline megastar would never have allowed (see page 104). And did you guess that Fraser had put the missing photo in there? That was why he kept trying to move the basket later, searching for a chance to get the photo out and throw it away safely. Did you spot that Fraser's ring was the same as the one worn by Bob Swing? It first appeared on page 103, then throughout the book. It should have given you a clue that they were the same person. And did you spot Fraser's handwriting on the script and the news clipping on page 125?

There were lots of clues to the identity of the mystery kidnapper who left the Spotlight Gang. Jack's notebook on page 120 mentioned that Luke's parents had a circus. No wonder he was able to run along a narrow branch over a waterfall in the dramatic rescue of Minnie Marvel! His agile rescue of Frankie Donaldson's kite on page 132 was another clue. On page 137, there was a final big hint in the news from Sam Smarm in the Publicity Department of Qualivision.

Did you work out the blackmail plot? On page 106, Thea mentioned Fraser's recent visit to his sister, and if you weren't sure that she was Elsa Storey, the Qualitime quiz confirmed it. All the ads in Qualitime were addressed to 'Dan' – Luke's name in Workout. On page 107 Thea mentioned how bad Luke's acting had been that Monday – the day he would have read the first ad in Qualitime. And on page 131, Jack's notebook mentions that the poison is Mythikan. The two people with a Mythikan connection were Fraser and Luke.

There were plenty of clues that Fraser stole the photos. First, there was his leaking pen. If you look closely at the subway ticket to Paparazzi Park station, you will see an ink blot on that, too. And Fraser was the only person who would have had time to get to the printers before they closed. Did you work out that Bella was Ed's daughter, Arabella, by his marriage to actress Posy Bouquet (see page 103)? So that would explain his choice of headlines on page 130!

First published in 1993 by Usborne Publishing Ltd, Usborne House, 83-85 Saffron Hill, London EC1N 8RT, England.
Copyright © 1994 Usborne Publishing Ltd.

The name Usborne and the device 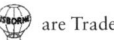 are Trade Marks of Usborne Publishing Ltd.

Printed in Great Britain   U.E.
First published in America August 1994